Sally Anderson
Living with Secrets

By Irene Martinez

Copyright © 2024

ISBN: 978-1-9999220-4-7

First Edition

Acknowledgements

I would sincerely like to thank the following people for their help in the completion of this book.

I would like to thank my son Jose Nunez Cole, who spent a lot of time and effort in the creation of the front and back cover and transposing the book into Print and Digital eBook.

The Doll Sally belonged to my sister Valerie who had downs Syndrome. My mother bought Sally for her after the second world war and she remained with my family until the death of my parents and sister Valerie. During the clearance of my parents' home, I decided to take Sally so she wouldn't be thrown away. And she became the best present my sister left me and became the inspiration for the Sally Anderson series of books.

Sally Anderson my Inspiration

2

Contents

1. Being Lucinda's Doll   5

2. The Auction   9

3. Mrs. Brown Dies   15

4. The Anderson Family   18

5. The Attic   21

6. Brigadier Anderson's Ghost   23

7. Amandas Sixteenth Birthday   26

8. The Bike Accident   28

9. My Friend Dies   30

10. The Funeral   34

11. I'am a Girl   38

12. The Orphanage   43

13. Holly and the Andersons   47

14. Greendale Forest   50

15. The Fight   54

16. December in the Orphanage   58

17. Christmas Events   64

18. Boxing Day   70

19. Langley Ewing's Haunted House   73

20. Terrorized by Birds   76

21. Holly and Sally in the Attic   80

22. Returning to the Orphanage   85

23. Holly's Birthday   89

24. The Duke and Alaric Castle   92

25. Leaving the Orphanage   103

Chapter 1
Being Lucinda's Doll

I'm Sally Anderson, and the story that I'm going to tell you is mine, about a wish I made which came true. I wasn't always a girl; I began my existence as a doll in an antique shop owned by Mr. Banham. The shop sold a variety of antique items, as well as unusual toys and dolls. I had been sitting on a shelf in the shop for several months, waiting for someone to come in and buy me. Then, one wet wintery afternoon, a man came into the shop to buy a present for his daughter's birthday, and I was sold to Mr. Somerfield. He put me into a box and laid me on the back seat of his car, which he drove to Hazelmere Drive, where he lived with his family. This was my first experience of living with a family and being someone's doll.

After opening the front door, he carried me into my new home, and from then on, a variety of frightening things began to take place. Once my box was unwrapped and I was taken out of it on Lucinda's birthday, I found her to be a nice little girl at first. She had long, jet-black hair arranged in curls around her oval-shaped face, and her eyes were a strange greenish colour that I grew to fear over time. When her eyes flashed with anger during her tempers, it frightened me. That nice little girl would transform into an aggressive, evil one who enjoyed finding ways to destroy me when we were alone in her bedroom.

During the first week of being her doll, she appeared to like me, but her attitude changed soon after her birthday. Whenever she took me up to her bedroom and closed the door, she'd throw me onto the bed, grab my arms and legs, and shake me non-stop, laughing hysterically. That was the beginning of the atrocious games she'd play with me once the door was shut. Sometimes she'd try to break my head off by twisting it, and she'd repeat the same antics with my arms and legs. Playing these types of games amused her, along with poking her fingers in my glass eyes, which was awful for me. Whenever her mother came into the bedroom and caught her doing this, she'd stop her with a slap.

During the time I spent with Lucinda as her doll, I learned a great deal about her terrible tantrums and what she could do to me. On those frightful days, all hell would break loose when she couldn't get her way. She'd stamp her feet and scream nonstop, and her temper would grow worse if she was sent up to bed early. On those occasions, her attacks on me were ferocious, and I'd end up with my arms and legs hanging from my body. The next day, her father would mend my damaged parts. When she started school, I felt relieved to be left alone with the other toys in the bedroom while she was out of the house. I'm sure the other toys were terrified of her too, as she'd made attempts to break them when she was in a bad mood. So, I dreaded her return from school each day.

And invented a game to play when I was left alone in the bedroom, called "Escape from Lucinda." It consisted of planning ways to get away from her if the opportunity arose. I hoped that she'd take me to the park and leave me behind, and another child would find me and take care of me. My plan never took place, as she stopped taking me to the park and went alone on her bike.

Things hadn't changed for me during the first year with the Somerfield family until one evening when her father returned home from work, and there was a quarrel between her parent's downstairs, with a great deal of loud shouting. The door of the living room was open, and I heard her mother crying and telling Lucinda, "Go up to your room and stay there." I heard her coming upstairs, the door opened, then slammed shut. Next, she walked over to where I was sitting on a chair, grabbed me, threw me onto the floor, and screamed several times, "I hate you," which scared me. She was in a temper, her eyes flashing with anger as she stared at me lying on the floor.

6

Then suddenly, I felt the pressure of her weight as she stamped on my head, and a sickening feeling as it broke in two. She then leaned down, grabbed me off the floor, and shook me again, my smashed head rattling. I thought, "Please don't hurt me; I'm your doll. Why do you want to break me?" My head was shattered, dangling from my body as she swung me around, laughing hysterically, while her parents' arguing grew louder downstairs. The other toys watched from the toy box, terrified, wondering what she'd do next.

An overwhelming silence covered the bedroom for a few moments, then footsteps coming upstairs. The door opened, and her mother came in, looking tearful. She sat on the bed and asked Lucinda to join her, saying, "Start behaving yourself and stop your tantrums. Your father's lost his job at the bank; we might have to move to another house." She kissed her, saying, "Go to bed and sleep." Once her mother left, she punched me several times and threw me into the toy box. When she was asleep, the other toys huddled around me, too frightened to speak in case she heard them. Toys can talk and be your friend when you're frightened.

Over the next few weeks, Lucinda's mother began to sort things out around the house, putting items into boxes ready to move. I wasn't played with anymore, as my head was smashed and I was left in the toy box. I wondered what would happen to me when the family moved; would I be thrown away? The answer came a few days later when Lucinda returned home from school and came up to the bedroom with her mother. Their conversation was mainly about school, and she said, "I'm glad to be leaving that school; I never liked it or the children there." Her mother knew why because the headmistress had given her detention quite a few times after school, so she was glad to be rid of her.

There were just a few days left before the family moved when I heard Lucinda coming upstairs to the bedroom. I was panic-stricken with fear of what she might do to me. The doorknob turned, and she came into the bedroom, walked over to the toy box, and threw us all onto the floor, saying, "I'll teach you all a lesson. I don't want old ragged toys with broken arms and legs or without eyes. I'm going to throw you all away." She began to kick us around the room. She stopped suddenly and said, "I don't need any of you," and threw us into a black bag, saying, "You're all going when the rubbish collection that comes on Friday." After saying that, she danced around the room, waving her arms in the air, singing and saying repeatedly, "You'll be at the rubbish dump on Friday to be ground up and burnt."

I'd heard terrible stories about what happens once you're taken to the rubbish dump in a black bag. You're squashed into little pieces and burnt. It was dark inside the black bag, and I clung to the other toys, frightened, having thoughts about the terrible things that were going to happen at the rubbish dump. If they did, my dream of being a girl would never come true. I was a broken doll at that time, who nobody wanted, frightened, lying inside a black bag that I couldn't escape from.

On Friday morning, I heard the rubbish collection lorry arrive and huddled closer to the other toys in the black bag. It began to rain, and the rain was falling onto the bag we were in. I heard the front door open. Had Lucinda come out of the house to say goodbye to us? She shouted in a loud voice to the man who took our bag away, "I hope my rubbish gets squashed into little pieces by the grinder and burnt." It was pouring with rain by then, as we were thrown onto the lorry, and I heard her say, "Bye-bye, rubbish bag of broken toys."

Chapter 2
The Auction

I was anxious as we drove away from the house and throughout the journey to the rubbish dump, hoping we wouldn't be squashed by the grinder. On arrival, our black bag was unloaded off the lorry and thrown onto a pile of bags, leaving us lying upside down. Then, a man picked up our bag and remarked, 'This bag is full of toys that could be saved for the jumble sale on Saturday.' Another man said, 'That's a good idea,' and closed the bag. What a relief, our bag wasn't going to be put on the rubbish pile. The following day, it was put in a car and taken to the church hall where the jumble sale was being held. We remained there for a few days, lying on the floor.

Until a lady opened the bag and said, 'Oh, this bag is full of toys.' She began taking us out of the bag and putting us on a table. While she was doing this, she noticed that I was broken and said, 'This doll needs a new head; it's smashed.' A woman replied, 'We could get a new head for her at the doll's hospital. What do you think, Mabel?' She replied, 'Let's do that, and we can sell her at a dolls auction for charity.' Mabel then placed me on another table while the other toys were being priced with labels for the jumble sale. Being separated from the other toys made me sad, but after my head was mended, things began to improve for me.

On the day Mabel took me to be repaired at the doll's hospital, I was scared. 'But who cares what a broken doll feels like?' On arrival at the doll's hospital, she handed me to a man who said he'd find a suitable head for me. He asked, 'What colour hair would you like for the doll?' Mabel said, 'Blonde hair and blue eyes.' My head was replaced, and my body mended. A few days later, Mabel came to get me from the doll's hospital, took me home with her, and dressed me in new clothes with underwear, a dress, shoes, and socks. Then she put me on the dressing table in her bedroom. The following day, she put me into a large box, and we left by car for a dolls auction, where she hoped someone would buy me.

On arrival at the auction, I was handed to a lady who opened my box and took me out. She looked at me carefully, nodded, and said to Mabel, 'This doll should sell at a good price as she's different.' Then she placed me on a large table with a variety of other dolls, all beautiful with lovely dresses of silk and satin. My clothes were plain compared to theirs. The lady auctioneer touched my cheek and whispered, 'You're a doll with a rare quality.'

Gradually, the hall began to fill with people until everyone was seated. Then an announcement from the auctioneer who spoke on a microphone, saying, 'I'll explain how the bidding with offers works,' and went through the process. The gavel struck the table, and she said, 'The auction begins now and will take offers for the Victorian dolls selection first.' That part of the auction went on for an hour until all the dolls were sold.

Then she came over to the table where I was standing with dolls from around the world. She pointed at me and said, 'The bidding starts now for this beautiful doll, with the first offer of £5.' No one responded. She didn't stop but continued asking for bids, and people began to respond by raising their hands with offers. On reaching £20 from a gentleman who raised his hand, the offer wasn't accepted, and the bidding continued until it reached £80. The hall was silent for a few moments, and I wondered who'd eventually own me. Then the auctioneer spoke, asking for the last bid of £100, and a lady's hand shot up from the back of the hall, shouting, 'I want her.' The gavel hit the table with a loud bang, and I was sold to Mrs. Tilly Brown.

She came over to the auctioneer while I was being packed into a box, patted my cheek, and said, 'My granddaughter Rosemary is going to love you.'

Mrs. Brown carried me out of the auction hall to a waiting taxi, and we left for Pinkerton Drive in the suburbs of London. On arrival at her house, she carried my box to the front door and rang the bell. Her granddaughter Rosemary opened the front door and said, 'Oh, you've been shopping again.' Grandma laughed and handed the box to Rosemary, saying, 'I hope you like her, dear.' She tore the paper off the box, opened it quickly, took me out, and kissed me. Rosemary was a cute little girl dressed in a school uniform with long blond hair tied in bunches. After kissing and hugging me, she thanked Grandma for buying me.

That night, Grandma took me up to Rosemary's bedroom and placed me next to her, saying, 'You don't have to be afraid of the dark anymore because now you have a friend, this lovely doll, Sally.' She kissed her goodnight, turned the light off, and left. Rosemary cuddled me and gradually drifted off to sleep. That was the first night we spent together, and I felt happy. Rosemary was five years old when I came to live with them. Over the next few months, everything ran smoothly. I was left in the bedroom during the day and taken downstairs by Grandma before Rosemary returned from school.

Over the next few months, everything was okay until the night when Grandma mentioned that she'd heard noises around the house. Before kissing Rosemary goodnight, she said, 'Don't worry if you hear anything during the night, call me.' She turned the light off and left. Rosemary gave me a hug and drifted off to sleep. During the night, noises began taking place outside the bedroom door that sounded like something being dropped. Rosemary woke up suddenly while the noise was going on and started to cry. She got out of bed, opened the door, and saw a pile of sweets lying on the floor in front of the door. Not knowing what to do, she grabbed me off the bed and ran into Grandma's bedroom, which was next door.

Grandma was already awake when Rosemary ran into her room. She picked her up quickly, put her in bed with her, and placed me on a chair next to her bed. She spoke to her granddaughter, saying, 'Don't be afraid, it was probably Mrs. Wright, the housekeeper who lived here once.' Rosemary asked, 'What did she do?' Grandma replied, 'She looked after the children for Councillor Applebee and his wife when they lived here. It was probably her who paid you a visit and left the sweets. She'd never harm you or Sally.' After being reassured by Grandma, Rosemary was calmer. Grandma went downstairs to make them some hot chocolate, returned quickly with their drinks, and they drank them and went back to sleep.

The following evening, when we went to bed, Grandma came into Rosemary's bedroom to read her a story before she went to sleep. That night, the story was about a scarecrow who lived in the village of Bloomingdale. He'd been put in one of the fields of Farmer Evans to frighten the birds away from his crops of wheat. As Grandma read the description of the scarecrow's appearance, it was scary! He was tall, wearing an old black baggy suit. His head was made of straw, with an old battered hat on it. His face was covered with a strange mask, and the eyes were painted orange with black circles. Everyone from the village who'd seen him at night said, 'His eyes glowed like burning fire in the darkness.'

That's why the people of Bloomingdale were terrified of seeing him on cold wintery nights when he'd appear from out of nowhere in the streets or lanes. There were rumours of him being able to morph into various frightening disguises and appear suddenly in front of you or behind you, especially at night when darkness engulfed the village. This frightened people from being out alone once night descended on the village; it turned into a creepy place.

One of the scarecrow's disguises was of an old woman who was grotesque, with a gaunt yellowish face covered with black moles. Her mouth was large, with two sharp glowing teeth protruding from either side of the lips. The hair that surrounded the freakish face was scraggly and greyish, flowing down her shoulders like a cape. People told tales of her appearing from out of the mist, cackling with weird laughter. These frightening apparitions seemed to happen during wintertime when a misty fog would rise from the ground and surround the village.

During that time of year, everyone who worked in the village square in the post office, grocery, or variety of shops would hurry home quickly after work. The headmistress of the village school, Miss Pricilla Peabody, who'd never married, had a bad temper and always carried a rolled-up umbrella throughout the year, come rain or shine. She boasted that if she caught the scarecrow in any of his disguises, she'd teach him a good lesson that he'd never forget. The children from the village school knew what she meant, as she often caned them with a large stick for the slightest bad behaviour. So, scarecrow would get a whacking from her if she ever caught him. Rosemary yawned, and Grandma said, 'I'll finish reading you the rest of the story tomorrow night.' She tucked her in bed, put me next to her, and turned off the light.

The following evening, Grandma continued reading the story to us, which grew even scarier when the scarecrow began getting up to his tricks. He looked through people's windows at night and appeared in trees in the lanes of Bloomingdale. In the last part of the book, he ends up being burnt in the field on a winter's night. No one owned up to doing this, but someone lit the match that brought an end to his antics. This gave the people of Bloomingdale the freedom to walk the streets and lanes at any time of year. We both listened to the story until Grandma finished the book. The picture on the cover of the book was scary, of the scarecrow burning in a field with his eyes lit up with flames of fire burning through the cover of the book. It left a frightening image. Rosemary held me even tighter that night until she fell asleep.

Chapter 3
Mrs. Brown Dies

I lived with Mrs. Brown and Rosemary until her eleventh birthday. Then, things drastically changed one afternoon when Grandma had a nasty fall while gardening and was taken to the hospital. Upon her return home, a lady began coming to clean the house and take care of Grandma, as she couldn't do the housework anymore. Rosemary was busy with homework every evening, leaving no time to play with me anymore. She seemed to have lost interest in me, her doll, and I wondered if she might decide to give me away. I was left in the bedroom every day, wondering what was going to happen to me.

The years had passed quickly since I'd arrived at Pinkerton Drive. Rosemary had gradually grown up, and on weekends, her school friends came around, and I wasn't played with anymore. During that year, Grandma's health gradually deteriorated, and she became worse, with the doctor visiting the house frequently. One morning, she woke up feeling ill, was taken to the hospital again, and died from a heart attack. Rosemary was inconsolable after her death, crying continuously over the following weeks. On the day of Grandma's funeral, she refused to eat altogether. The house was full of people, and the sound of their voices drifted upstairs. I missed Grandma too.

About a week after Mrs. Brown's funeral, Rosemary returned to school, and Aunt Dorothy arrived to arrange the sale of the house. It was going to be sold, and Rosemary was going to live with her aunt. Grandma had left sufficient money for Rosemary's care and future education. Things changed when Aunt Dorothy arrived, from then on, I was an item of no use and totally disregarded. Rosemary missed Grandma after her sudden death and continued to cry often at night.

Over the following weeks, everything was in constant turmoil with people coming to view the house, along with things being packed into boxes and trunks, with her aunt in control of everything. Rosemary had no time for me, and I knew the happy years we'd spent together were over. One morning, Aunt Dorothy came into Rosemary's bedroom to start clearing it and began by putting her toys and books into black bags. She came over to where I was sitting on a chair, looked at me, and said, "You'll have to go." That's how it ended for me, being Rosemary's doll at Pinkerton Drive.

Next, the house was cleared quickly for the new owners, who were arriving and moving in once Aunt Dorothy and Rosemary left for their new home. "What was going to happen to me?" The answer came when Aunt Dorothy took me from the chair and threw me into a bag. For the second time, I was in a black bag as a doll that wasn't wanted, and left in the hall. Later that day, a charity shop van arrived to collect some items of furniture, along with me. Just before I was taken to the van, I heard Rosemary say to her aunt, "I hope someone nice buys Sally," and she patted the bag I was in, saying, "Goodbye, Sally." I wasn't wanted again and was alone in the bag, crying as the van drove away from Pinkerton Drive to the charity shop.

After a short journey, the van stopped, and the driver got out to unload the van. My bag was taken off first and put in the sorting room of the shop. Some ladies were talking when the man put my bag down on the floor. I heard one of them say, "I wonder what's inside that black bag?" Someone picked the bag up, opened it, and a lady took me out, saying to another woman, "It's a large doll. She looks valuable. Let's tell the manager about her." Daisy called the manager, who arrived to have a look at me and agreed that I could be valuable. She then phoned some dealers who value dolls to see if any of them were interested in buying me.

That evening, when the shop closed, all the lights were turned off, and I was left alone in the sorting room. In the dark, it was creepy, and I felt scared, wishing Mrs. Wright would visit me. The silence was broken by a light swishing noise, a flash of light, and Mrs. Wright appeared. "Hello, Sally, where's Rosemary?" I wanted to answer but couldn't and nodded. Puzzled, she said, "Make a wish that you can talk." I did and wished. She asked again, "How are you, dear?" I spoke, saying, "Really sad and lonely." She replied, "Everything is going to be alright." I asked, "Will you visit me again?" "I will, Sally, never fear," and she vanished with a flash of light, leaving me alone in the dark.

The next day, the manager put me on display in the shop. I hadn't been there long when a tall man with fair hair, dressed in black, came into the shop. He looked at some of the dolls on the shelves, then came over to look at me and asked Daisy, "How much is this doll?" She didn't know and went to ask the manager, who came back a few minutes later and said, "The doll's going to be valued before she's sold." He left his card and said, "Let me know the price of the doll once she's been valued, as I'm interested in buying her."

Once he left the shop, the manager phoned various experts to have me valued so I could be sold. Over the next few days, I was taken to different people who prodded and looked at me from every angle until they all agreed I could be sold for at least one hundred pounds. After receiving this information, the manager began to phone various people who might be interested in buying me and phoned the man who'd left his card with Daisy.

Chapter 4
The Anderson Family

The following day, after a phone call from the manager, the tall man dressed in black came back into the shop. The manager spoke with him, and he came over to have another look at me. He wrote a cheque, and I was sold to Mr. Anderson as a present for his daughter. Packed into a box, and carried out of the charity shop by Mr. Anderson, who, upon reaching his car, opened the door and placed me on the back seat. After a long drive, we arrived at our destination. He took my box out of the car and carried me up a path that led to his house, which would become my new home.

There was a shriek of delight from a small girl as he opened the front door. She exclaimed, "Oh daddy, you do spoil me!" My box was pulled open by a chubby pair of hands, and I was taken out by Amanda. She looked at me and said to her father, "Wow, she's gorgeous!" That's how I met Amanda for the first time and became her doll. She had bright reddish hair, a cute little face with large blue eyes, and she giggled and kissed her father, who gave her a hug while she held me. Next, she attempted to stand me upright, saying, "Oh, isn't she big, and she looks like a real girl with those blue eyes. Where did you get her?" Her father replied, "From the charity shop. She's valuable and antique, so take good care of her, as she's an investment, not a toy."

Amanda was careful and did look after me from the moment I became her doll. She said to her father, "I'll put her in the lounge and find somewhere else later. What's her name?" He replied, "There was a label on her from her previous owner. It's Sally." "Oh, I like that," she said with a mischievous grin, one that I got used to seeing over the years. She was seven years old when I came to live with the family.

The Andersons lived in a large detached Victorian house named Whispering Echoes. It had two floors, with a staircase in the centre of the house made of brown mahogany that led to the second floor. On the landing of the second floor, there was a narrow flight of winding stairs that led to an attic. Amanda's parents had already warned her not to go up there, and she often wondered how many secrets lay hidden in the mysterious attic. All the stairs in the house creaked whenever they were walked on, creating a creepy atmosphere. The windows of the building had dark green shutters that were kept closed most of the time. The large garden surrounding the house was full of plants, shrubs, and large trees, which created an odd, strange atmosphere when night descended on the garden.

Mr. Anderson was a funeral director, and his wife owned a ladies' clothes shop in the centre of town. Sometimes Amanda's father brought certain jobs home from his funeral business that he had to finish. On those occasions, he'd be working late in the basement of the house, preparing deceased people before families came to visit them in the funeral chapel. He was a qualified makeup artist and embalming specialist who took pride in his work.

One evening soon after I'd arrived, Amanda's father was working late in the basement, and she carried me down there with her to watch him work. It was strangely fascinating to see him transform deceased people into looking alive again once he applied makeup. Amanda sat watching him attentively until he said, "Amanda, I've told you not to come down here while I'm working. It's out of bounds for you, do you understand?" "Yes, I haven't been here long," she replied. "Go upstairs with Sally, and don't come down here again."

She left the basement carrying me and made her way upstairs to the lounge where her mother was watching TV. On seeing Amanda, her mother said, "I hope you haven't been in the basement. You're not allowed to go there when your father is working down there. Go and get ready for bed now. I'm not happy with you; there's no TV for the rest of the week until you learn to do what you're told." Amanda didn't reply but went over to her mother, kissed her goodnight, and left with me for upstairs.

From my first night in the house, Amanda insisted that I should be with her and put me in a glass cabinet in her bedroom. I liked being in the cabinet, as I could watch her throughout the night. Most nights she slept peacefully, but that night she woke up screaming from a nightmare. Her mother heard her and came rushing into the bedroom to see what was wrong. Amanda explained that some of the deceased people she'd seen in the basement were talking to her and coming into her bedroom. Her parents reassured her that those people couldn't harm her and that she wasn't allowed to go down to the basement anymore. They emphasized that she must listen to what they say for her own good.

Chapter 5
The Attic

It was close to Christmas, and Amanda was home on a two-week holiday from school. Her parents were both out at work that day, with her mother expected to return home at lunchtime. I remember the mischievous grin on her face when she took me out of the cabinet and said, "We're going to explore the attic, Sally, and I've got the key. I knew where my father kept it."

After she said that, a gust of cold air blew through the landing where we were standing. She clung to me suddenly, looking at the flight of stairs that led to the attic. Then, carrying me, she made her way up the narrow, winding staircase to the top, where a large door confronted us. She hesitated, then put me on the floor against the wall and took a key out of her skirt pocket to open the door. The key didn't budge at first, but on the second attempt, it turned in the lock, and the door swung open with a screeching sound.

Amanda picked me up, and we went into the attic. After entering, the door slammed shut behind us with a loud bang. She was nervous, and her grip tightened around me as she stood in total darkness holding me. She then spoke, saying, "There are lights up here somewhere, but I don't know where they are." She put me down on the floor again and stumbled around in the dark until she found the light switch, and turned the lights on. The attic was large, with cobwebs hanging down from the roof, and a few paintings of people whose eyes seemed to be staring at you hung on the walls. There was a lot of old furniture and various oddments of things that weren't being used anymore. Amanda loved having this exciting adventure in this creepy place that was out of bounds for her by her parents.

As we stood in silence in the dim attic light, a swishing noise began coming from one of the corners of the attic. Then a flash of white light appeared, and a transparent image of Mrs. Wright appeared near us. Her sudden arrival brought a scream from Amanda. The woman spoke to her, saying, "Don't be afraid. I'm Mrs. Wright, and I know what mischievous children do, like you, Amanda, disobeying your parents again and coming up to the attic." While she was speaking, various weird noises were taking place throughout the attic. Mrs. Wright shouted, "Be gone!" and the noises stopped. Amanda was terrified upon hearing them and mentioned to the woman that she had been hearing voices. Mrs. Wright replied, "They can't harm you. Tell them to go. I appeared to help you as the attic door is locked." After saying that, she went over to the door, touched it, and the door swung open. Then she disappeared.

Amanda grabbed me quickly, and we went through the open door, which shut behind us with a bang. Carrying me, she made her way downstairs quickly and managed to get back to her bedroom before her mother arrived home from work at lunchtime. Once we were in her bedroom, she put me back in the glass cabinet. That's when I saw my reflection in the mirror of the dressing table. I did look like a girl but wasn't one. After our adventure in the attic, Amanda slept much better at night and stopped talking about the voices. Although the spirit for adventure remained with her, she was eager to explore the attic again.

Chapter 6
Brigadier Anderson's Ghost

The seasons gradually changed from winter to spring, then into the warmer days of summer. During that time, Amanda was busy with her school friends and wasn't at home on her weekends from school, but always out somewhere. Then autumn returned, with darker days and cold nights, which changed the house into a dismal, gloomy place once the shutters were closed at night.

Even the garden was uninviting, as the trees had shed their leaves around the garden that surrounded the house. Amanda began a new term at school, with plenty of homework to do each afternoon when she returned home, which she did until her mother served their evening meal.

While they were having dinner on one of those evenings, I noticed that she seemed impatient for the meal to end. When it finally did, her parents went into the lounge to watch TV, while she left quickly for the hall to get the key for the attic. She came back quickly, holding the key with a mischievous grin, picked me up, and we began to make our way up the winding staircase that led to the attic. After she'd been warned again not to go up there, why was she disobeying her parents' warning? We were halfway upstairs when a weird supernatural force took hold, pulling us towards the attic. When the stairs ended, we were standing on the landing, facing the mysterious door again.

Amanda was excited, as she was on the verge of another adventure. She stared at the door for a few seconds, put me down on the floor, and opened the door. This time, when she put the key in the lock and turned it, the door opened with a loud creaking noise. She picked me up, and we went into the attic.

This time, she found the light switch quickly, pressed it down, and a dim light came on, covering the attic. Feeling frustrated, she stamped her feet, and a shrill piercing sound filled the semi-darkness as the attic door slammed shut. The lights flickered, got dimmer, until we were in complete darkness. Then we heard rustling, followed by a squeaking noise close to where we were standing. The atmosphere was tense and overbearing when something fell with a loud crash. Amanda was shaking as an oppressive silence filled the attic. A large rat scurried across the floor, touched Amanda, and she screamed! We were alone; there was no one to help us.

Fumbling around in the dark, she made another attempt to switch the lights on, and they came on with a dim light, which shone onto a portrait of a man in uniform on a trunk close to where she was standing. In the dim light, his eyes seemed to move and be staring at us. Amanda saw the eyes move and was scared stiff. Her curiosity had led us to another frightening situation. At that moment, another shadowy shape of a large rodent ran across the floor near us. It didn't touch her, but she shrieked, "Get away from me," as its long tail swept across the floor and out of sight. While this was taking place in the attic, her parents were downstairs watching TV. So, if she screamed for help, no one would hear her. I remained sitting on the floor, where she'd left me.

Amanda was desperate. She ran towards the door, tried to open it, and couldn't. In despair, she sat on the trunk next to the painting and began to cry. While she was doing this, the man in the portrait spoke to her, saying, "Can't you understand what you've done again, coming up to the attic after you've been told not to?" She was dumbstruck on hearing his voice and stopped crying. He spoke again and said, "You've opened a wormhole that could lead to disaster. I'm Brigadier Anderson, an ancestor of yours, who owned this house for many years. I died on the battlefield in the Crimean War. I loved this house and was drawn back to it." Amanda asked, "Are you always here in the attic?" He replied, "I'm here in spirit and remain quietly in the attic, as this was my home. When your parents come up to the attic, they never cause any bother, but your mischievous ways will bring trouble." She asked, "How can I get out of here? The door won't open." He replied, "You should have thought about that before you came up here."

She pleaded with him, saying, "Please help me. I must get back to my bedroom before my parents notice that I'm not there." Smiling, he said, "Try clapping your hands, stamping your feet, saluting me, then go to the door, put the key in the lock, and turn it. If the door opens, leave and never return. Do you understand?" "Yes, Brigadier." He nodded and said, "Let's begin and see what happens." Instantly, Amanda began to clap her hands, stamp her feet, ran to the door, put the key in the lock, turned it, and the door opened with a squeaking sound. The Brigadier was enjoying this nonsense and laughing as we went through the door, where she paused to look back at him. He winked, the lights went off, and the door closed behind us, squeaking.

Chapter 7
Amandas Sixteenth Birthday

The years passed by quickly, and Amanda never stopped getting herself into scrapes throughout her teenage years. By that time, she considered me to be her best friend, someone she could confide in, who never told her what to do. Occasionally, she'd come up to me and give me a kiss when things were going well for her, which wasn't often. I remember her sixteenth birthday well, and her parents being busy making arrangements for her birthday party, as she'd invited quite a few of her school friends. Her mother was having a dress made for her in London, which arrived at the shop that morning, and they drove into town to collect it.

Upon their arrival back home, her mother went to fix lunch, and Amanda had some spare time before it was ready. That mischievous look appeared on her face, and I knew she wanted to visit the attic again. She hadn't been up there since Brigadier Anderson had warned her not to. I couldn't understand why she kept wanting to go there after being warned so many times. She was sixteen on that birthday and thought nothing could harm her. When she grabbed me suddenly, got the key from the hall, and we were making our way up the winding staircase again. Amanda put the key in the lock of the attic door; this time, it opened with a grinding sound.

On entering the attic, a grey mist was rising from the floor while she searched for the light switch. Finally, she found it, the lights flickered, and came on. The mist clung to the clumps of cobwebs that hung down from the rafters of the roof. There was also a pungent smell of decay from the old objects stored there. Amanda stood gazing at the mist as it rose from the floor, surrounding us, becoming a swirling ball of moving mist with life-like shapes forming inside of it. Freakish noises began from different parts of the attic as more transparent images morphed into weird shapes around us, horrifying to see. The alien forms made strange wailing noises as they moved closer to where we were. Amanda turned deathly white, went hysterical, and said, 'What are they?' There was no one to help us, as the brigadier's painting had been moved. So, we were alone facing this terrifying situation. The ghostly images began to manifest more intensely in the attic, accompanied by unbearably loud, strange noises.

As the mist moved closer towards us, we could see the distorted images inside of it, and the attic turned freezing cold. Amanda had left her jacket downstairs and shivered as goose pimples covered her arms. The whole experience was terrifying and unbelievable, but it was happening. Amanda was paralyzed where she stood, too frightened to move. As the ghostly shapes got closer to her, they made horrible moaning sounds that grew louder upon reaching her and making contact with her body. She was in a catatonic state when the phantom manifestation of ghosts went through her body. She didn't move and seemed rooted to where she stood, petrified, and traumatized by the nightmarish ordeal she was experiencing.

The ghosts left behind a greyish slimy matter covering the floor and Amanda's entire body, which was still and lifeless. The atmosphere in the attic was dead silent until Amanda began to cry uncontrollably, picked me up from the floor, and clung to me in shock. Still traumatized, she let out a piercing scream, then went berserk, running around the attic. While she was doing this, a large rat ran across her feet. She screamed, kicking it across the floor, tripped over, and fell against the attic wall. This caused a hidden partition to begin to open with a loud scraping noise. Seeing the gap in the wall, her grip on me tightened as she went through the gap carrying me, and down a flight of narrow stairs until they ended. A door confronted her, and she kicked it open, leading to the garden at the back of the house. Then she went through the kitchen and up to her bedroom.

Chapter 8
The Bike Accident

When her mother called her for lunch, Amanda went to the kitchen and didn't mention anything about what had taken place in the attic. That day felt strange, and during lunch, her mother began to speak about the house and its history. Amanda listened attentively as her mother recounted stories of people who had visited the house, claiming to have seen mystifying images on the staircase and heard strange noises coming from the attic.

After lunch, Amanda made an excuse about needing to visit the library to get some books for a school assignment. She said, "I won't be long," to her mother, grabbed her bike from the garage, and left for the library to get information about paranormal activities. Upon arrival at the library, she searched the shelves until she found some books on the subject to borrow.

Amanda left the library with the books and began cycling back home, a journey that would take about fifteen minutes. She was halfway home when a car coming towards her went out of control, spinning across the road straight in front of her. Amanda was thrown off her bike and into the air, ending up lying across another car, bleeding and unconscious. The police stopped the traffic, and she was taken to the hospital. Her parents were notified and were frantic with worry when they heard the news about her accident, spending the night at the hospital with her. The following morning, the doctor told them that Amanda needed an emergency operation to save her life.

The operation took place, and over the following months, Amanda gradually regained her health to a certain degree, but the accident affected her ability to walk up and down stairs for several months. Seeing her in this condition made me sad as I watched her daily from where I stood propped up against the wall. I wasn't human then and couldn't talk or say, "I'll always be your friend." After her accident, I became obsessed with the idea of becoming a girl and began to observe people more closely to see how they walked and spoke. I started to copy those things, hoping to become a human girl in the near future.

The days grew shorter as autumn approached again, with the garden full of leaves covering the lawn, making everything look gloomy and dull. The door we had escaped from the attic by was now kept locked. How many more secrets lay hidden up there behind the closed door? One night, there was a bad storm with rain gushing against the bedroom shutters nonstop. Amanda woke up that night sobbing after another nightmare with visions of people whispering to her. Her mother came into the bedroom, sat chatting with her for quite a while, then left for the kitchen to make her a hot drink. When she returned with their drinks, she sat with Amanda until she went back to sleep.

Chapter 9
My Friend Dies

After Christmas that year, Amanda was going to college, starting a new life as a student. She would be living away from home in student accommodation and coming home to see her parents every two weeks. Shortly after Christmas, arrangements were made for her to travel to the college, where she would be studying for the next couple of years. It was snowing on the day she left with her parents by car, embarking on her new life as a college student. Before leaving, she came over to me, gave me a kiss, and said, "I'll see you in a couple of weeks. Goodbye, Sally."

What would happen to me now? Would I be given away? That didn't happen, but something much worse did, a few months later, bringing vast changes for me and the Anderson family.

The house was quiet and lifeless without Amanda rushing around, and it was lonely without her at night in the bedroom. Her mother came up to clean her room once a week, and then I was left completely alone in silence again while Amanda was away at college. During that time, I practiced my walking daily, and it gradually improved. I began to feel sensations in my arms and legs when I moved. My next task was to learn how to talk, which I hadn't done since I'd spoken to Mrs. Wright and had forgotten how to do. So, I began by repeating sentences and was surprised when various different sounds came out of my mouth. And became more excited about being a human girl.

Mrs. Wright had said, "If you believe enough in something, it can turn into reality." I did, and gradually began to experience different signs as my transformation into a girl was taking place. My doll's body, made of hard plastic or China, gradually altered and became softer, like human skin. Next, I could open and close my eyes naturally and started to feel sensations in most of my doll's body as the changes took place.

The months passed by, and summer returned with warmer days. The garden was in full bloom, with flowers creating a tapestry of colour in the sunshine. Soon, Amanda would be coming home to spend her summer holidays from college with her parents. On the day she was due to arrive home, her mother was busy preparing things. She came up to the bedroom, picked me up to dust the chair I was sitting on, and noticed a few flakes of plastic had fallen off my body. She remarked, "Sally, your body's starting to flake. You feel much softer." After saying that, she put me back on the chair and left.

I was excited, waiting for Amanda to arrive home and rush upstairs to unpack her case. I wondered if she'd notice the changes in me. The hours passed by as I waited impatiently for her to arrive home, but there was no sign of her. And could hear her parents' talking downstairs, and they seemed worried about why Amanda hadn't arrived yet. Suddenly, the front doorbell rang. Amanda's mother went to answer the door. Someone was talking to her, then she screamed hysterically and started crying. Mr. Anderson said, "It can't be true. There must be a mistake." After a lot of talking and crying downstairs, Amanda's mum came rushing upstairs to get her coat, then went back down. The front door slammed, and the Andersons drove away in a hurry.

They didn't return that night and came back the following morning with Mrs. Anderson in a terrible state. Her husband helped her into the house and then upstairs to their bedroom, where she remained for the next few weeks, ill from the shock of Amanda's death. A doctor made several visits, and her husband walked about in a trance-like state, looking after her so she could get well. On the day the news came about Amanda being killed in a car crash, she'd been on her way home with a girlfriend from college who'd offered her a lift when the accident happened. I couldn't believe that she was dead and that I'd never see her again. The whole house went into mourning for her and was deadly silent. Everyone missed her enchanting personality, which always kept you guessing about what mischief she'd get up to next. On the night of her death, there was a summer storm with gusts of wind howling around the house, rattling the shutters of the bedroom windows. I missed her.

Throughout the next week, Amanda's mum stayed in their bedroom during the day while her husband went to work. Each evening, they'd have their dinner upstairs, then he'd help her downstairs to the lounge, where she never stayed long before returning to their bedroom. Things got better after Mr. Anderson phoned his mother and asked her to come stay with them for a couple of weeks. Once Gran arrived, she managed to get Mrs. Anderson to come downstairs during the day while she prepared their lunch. Afterwards, they'd go into the lounge for a chat and a cup of tea. Gran understood that her daughter-in-law was grieving the loss of her daughter and needed someone to talk to.

During the weeks that Gran was staying with the Andersons, my doll's body was rapidly transforming its appearance into a human girl, and I was completely alone while this was happening. No one came up to the bedroom anymore, and the door was kept locked, so I was cut off from the family. By chance one morning, I saw myself in the mirror and knew that my transformation from a doll into a girl was happening quickly. What would happen to me once I had changed completely? Would the Andersons keep me or send me away? If they did, I'd have nowhere to go. I sat on the floor and cried, with water coming out of my eyes.

While I was crying, the bedroom lights came on, and Mrs. Wright appeared surrounded by a shimmering white light. She smiled and said, "Come and give me a hug, Sally. Your wish is coming true."

She asked, "Would you like to stay with the Andersons or go somewhere else? Don't be afraid to tell me; you need a home now that you're a girl." I asked, "What should I do if someone comes into the bedroom?" She replied, "Remain still, don't move. I'll be back to see you soon. Bye, sweetie," and then vanished. The lights went off, and I was alone in the dark, wondering what would happen to me next.

Chapter 10
The Funeral

During the following week, people were coming and going, planning Amanda's funeral. Mr. Anderson brought his daughter's body home to be close to her parents a couple of days before the funeral, and she was put in the basement. I wanted to see her for the last time but couldn't get down there without being carried by someone. The house was completely quiet on the night before the funeral. The Andersons and Gran went into the lounge after their evening meal, and the silence was suddenly broken by the sound of footsteps coming upstairs that stopped outside the bedroom. The door was unlocked, and Amanda's mum came into the bedroom, took me off the chair, and held me tight. She then spoke, saying, "Sally, I want you to come to see my daughter for the last time, as she loved you."

She carried me down to the basement. On arrival, the door was open, and we went in. Amanda was lying in a beautiful coffin surrounded by white flowers, looking peaceful like she did at night when she slept. Her mother burst into tears, her father held back his, as they both went up to the coffin to kiss Amanda. Her mother then lowered me close to Amanda and said, "Sally's come to say goodbye, dear." I touched her cheek with my hand and thought, "I'll always love you." After our goodbyes, there was a freaky silence and a soft rustling sound from one of the corners of the basement, with a misty apparition of the brigadier, who'd come to say goodbye to Amanda. His image was only there for a few seconds before it faded.

On the day of the funeral, the Andersons were up early arranging everything, and Gran was in the kitchen preparing a buffet for after the funeral. I was still in the bedroom and managed to climb onto a chair by the window to watch the people arrive for the funeral. It was hard not to think about the previous night, and seeing Amanda for the last time. The clock in the hall struck midday, and the cars began to leave to take everyone to the church for the service, then on to the cemetery. Feeling lost and alone, I watched the scene from a chair by the window, longing to be with everyone, until the line of cars drove away, disappearing into the distance. Once everyone had left, the house was quiet. I walked over to the bed, sat on it, and cried for the loss of my friend.

The wind howled around the house and garden for the next few hours. The trees close to the bedroom window swayed and beat against the shutters. Everything seemed to mourn the loss of Amanda, as I did, on the day of the funeral. Although her spirit seemed to linger with me throughout that day. Later that afternoon, there was the sound of cars returning to the house after the funeral with people who'd been invited back for the buffet. So, I knew no one would be coming up to the bedroom. I walked over to the bed, pushed the duvet cover back, and climbed into bed. It was hard to believe that I was doing things Amanda had done, and gradually drifted to sleep. I had a dream while I slept, of Amanda who spoke to me and said, "Your wish is coming true to be a girl, Sally. I'll be around to help you," and the dream ended.

The house was silent for the next few days after the funeral, apart from occasional noises made by Gran when she was cleaning around the house. She did everything, including shopping, cooking, arranging meals, and answering the phone. Throughout that sad period, my transformation into a human was nearly complete. The reality of what was happening frightened me, as my doll's body gained mobility, and I got used to sleeping at night. Then one morning, I woke up and heard footsteps coming upstairs to the bedroom. Panicked, got out of bed quickly and back onto the chair where I was kept just before the door opened, and Gran came into the bedroom.

A weird atmosphere covered the room while Gran stood gazing at Amanda's things, and it was like she was waiting for her to appear. Gran then left to get the hoover and her cleaning things from the landing, came back, and started cleaning the room. When she changed the sheets of the bed, I was scared that she'd find some flakes of plastic that had fallen off and see the empty spaces on my doll's body if she picked me up. Nothing happened. She brushed the flakes of plastic into a dustpan and continued cleaning.

Once she'd finished cleaning the room, Gran sat on the bed and cried. She took me off the chair, saying, "Sally, Amanda loved you. I miss her," and hugged me. She sat on the bed and was looking at a photo of her granddaughter when the door opened, and Mrs. Anderson came in and sat next to Gran, saying, "Thanks for cleaning the room, I couldn't face doing it." Gran put me back on the chair and said, "Let's go and make a nice cup of tea," and they left for downstairs. Sitting on the chair again, I remembered how I'd nearly been caught that morning sleeping in the bed. I heard a faint giggle and a voice say, "My plan's working, Sally." That night I was scared to get into bed and slept on the chair.

Summer disappeared gradually, and autumn returned with darker days, and the whole house seemed empty without Amanda. Memories came flooding back from the past, and of our adventures in the attic. Once we opened that door, it led into a strange world of ghostly manifestations that lay hidden behind the attic door. My transformation took place rapidly after Amanda's death, with proof of what was happening when I looked in the mirror and saw myself as a small girl of about three years old with blonde hair and blue eyes. It was unbelievable, but my wish had come true to be a girl. I waved to the little girl; she waved back. It was me, and I wasn't Amanda's doll anymore. Would the Andersons keep me or send me away? The reality of what had taken place in my doll's body with its transformation was confusing. I was tired and tearful, got into bed, and slept.

Chapter 11
I'm a Girl

The following morning, I was woken up unexpectedly by Gran, who came into the bedroom to change the sheets again and found me sleeping in Amanda's bed. When she pulled the duvet cover back and saw me, she gasped in surprise and said, "What are you doing in my granddaughter's bed? This room's been kept locked." Then she bent down, picked me up, saw I was wearing my doll's clothes, and asked, "Where's Amanda's doll?" I nodded, and she asked, "Who are you, little girl? Can you talk?" She then sat me back on the bed and went to call Mrs. Anderson to come upstairs. When she returned, I tried to speak and say, "I'm Sally, don't you recognize me?"

Mrs. Anderson arrived quickly and asked her mother-in-law, "What's wrong?" She saw me sitting on the bed and said, "Who's this little girl?" Gran replied, "I found her in Amanda's bed when I came up to clean the room. She can't speak." Mrs. Anderson said, "We need to call the police and the children's placement service right away." She noticed I was wearing my doll's clothes, started to cry, and said, "What have they done with Sally?" Gran said, "Phone Ralph and tell him to come home; say it's an emergency." Mrs. Anderson left to call her husband.

On Mr. Anderson's arrival home, Gran repeated the full story of how I was found in Amanda's bedroom. He smiled at me, picked me up, and said, "You need something to eat and drink while we wait for the children's placement service to arrive." He then carried me downstairs to the lounge and asked Gran to fix something to eat for me. She left for the kitchen and came back quickly, carrying a tray with scrambled eggs, soft bread, and a glass of milk. That was the first time I ate food and drank liquid, something I had to learn to do as I was human now.

The placement service was phoned but was unable to come until Monday. After hearing that, the Andersons agreed to keep me until then, and Gran suggested going into town to buy some clothes for me so they could manage over the weekend. Mrs. Anderson remarked, "I wonder how old she is?" Gran replied, "She looks about three." Amanda's mum put me on her lap and fed me some scrambled eggs and bread. Once she'd finished feeding me, her husband took me from her, gave me a hug, and said, "You might be a blessing in disguise, sent to help us through this difficult time."

Gran returned later that afternoon from shopping in town with lots of clothes and various things children need. Once she was back, Mrs. Anderson went upstairs to make sure the bedroom was okay for me, while her husband went to the attic to get a cot for me to sleep in, which had been Amanda's. Since being found that morning, the Andersons had taken care of me, knowing this wouldn't last and that I'd be leaving them soon. An image of Amanda then appeared near me with a mischievous grin, gave me the thumbs up, and vanished.

The Andersons seemed happier that day looking after me and kept me downstairs with them that evening, sitting on the couch between them while they watched TV until it was time for bed. Mrs. Anderson took me upstairs to the bedroom, dressed me in pink pyjamas, gave me a drink, and put me into a small white bed, covering me up. She turned the light off and said, as they were leaving, "Do you think she'll be okay alone tonight?" Mr. Anderson replied, "We'll leave the door open in case she cries," and they left.

The following day was Sunday. Gran got me up early to bathe, dress me in new clothes, and feed me breakfast. When the Andersons came down for theirs, Mr. Anderson said to Gran, "We're visiting the Pattersons today, Mum, and taking the little girl with us. If anyone asks about her, she's a relative of the family who's staying with us."

After breakfast, Mr. Anderson carried me out to the car. I looked back at the bedroom window and saw the curtains move, also a faint image of someone watching us. Was it Amanda? Mr. Anderson opened the back door of the car and handed me over to Gran, who put me on the back seat next to her. Amanda's mum arrived, looking lovely that morning, wearing a blue suit with a matching hat, and got into the car smiling, happier than I'd seen her recently. That day was a wonderful experience of being with a family, as the following day I was leaving them. The placement service was coming to get me, and I'd never see the family again. That night, when Mrs. Anderson put me to bed, she looked unhappy and remained with me for some time before kissing me and turning the light off.

Gran got me up early the next day to bathe, dress me, and give me breakfast before the Andersons came downstairs for theirs. On their arrival in the kitchen, they didn't stop talking about the people from the children's placement service who were coming to get me that morning and seemed worried. While they were having breakfast, the front doorbell rang suddenly. Mr. Anderson got up from the table to answer the door, saying, "It's them come to get her." I started to cry. Mrs. Anderson picked me up and said, "Don't cry, they're going to find your parents. You'll be back with them soon." I put my arms around her neck and clung to her.

A few moments later, her husband came back into the kitchen, followed by the two people who'd come to collect me. The woman spoke first, saying, "I'm Miss Rebecca Crow, this is Mr. Bates, we're from children's placement services," and said to Mr. Bates, "Start taking information down. I want this done quickly." He then took a pen and pad out of his briefcase, ready to start writing. Miss Crow spoke to the Andersons and said, "We're going to ask some questions about the child you found in your home," and stared at me. Her face was white with a long-pointed nose, her lips were narrow and blood red. She was wearing high-heeled shoes that were pointed,

40

making her look ginormous. Her jet-black hair was pulled back in a bun on top of her head. Wow, she was scary. She reminded me of Lucinda when she pointed her bony finger at me and said, "So you're the child, can you speak?" I was too frightened to speak while she stared at me.

After a brief silence, she spoke to the Andersons again and said, "We're here to find a temporary place for this child until there's a permanent residence for her." While she was speaking, the other social worker was taking details down and began to question the family at length about how I was found in their daughter's bedroom. He asked some wild questions, suggesting the Andersons might have kidnapped me to replace the daughter that had recently died. Mr. Anderson was furious, lost his temper, and shouted at Mr. Bates, saying, "Do you think my wife and I would do such a terrible thing and kidnap another family's child?" Miss Crow looked at him with an accusing stare. Then at Mrs. Anderson, and said, "Get the child ready to leave. I don't have all day; we have a busy schedule."

Mrs. Anderson was lost for words, tears rolled down her face as she left to get my bag from the hall, which was already packed. Gran got up from the couch and said to Rebecca Crow, "Be careful what you're saying to my son and his wife. I'm a witness to what you're accusing them of. My daughter-in-law is getting over a nervous breakdown through the death of her daughter, so be careful." Then she left to make tea and returned quickly, carrying a tray with tea and cakes. Ignoring Miss Crow, she sat on the couch, put me on her lap, and fed me chocolate cake and milk.

Once everyone had tea, it was time to leave with Miss Crow, who watched me get off Gran's lap and said, "You're big enough to walk, I'm not carrying you." Mr. Anderson was controlling his temper. He picked me up and carried me out to Miss Crow's car, looking tense. The family kissed me goodbye, and he said, "I'll visit you wherever you're placed to make sure you're being looked after okay," and touched my cheek. I waved to the family that I'd grown to love over the days I'd spent with them. Miss Crow started the car, and we drove away from the Andersons' home.

During the long journey in the car, she turned to me and asked, "Do you want to go to the toilet? We'll stop if you do." I nodded, and she remarked, "I don't want a mess in my car," reminding me of Lucinda, who had returned to haunt me in the form of Miss Crow. She continued driving for some time, then stopped suddenly and said, "Get out," pointing to where there were toilets. I had never gone to the toilet alone; Gran had taken me during the time I'd spent with the Andersons and put me on the loo. Miss Crow stared at me and said, "Hurry up," and I toddled off in the direction where she was pointing.

When I reached the toilets, I couldn't reach the handle of the door to open it, I was too small. After pushing the door several times, it opened. I went in and ended up peeing on the floor as I couldn't climb onto the toilet seat and fell, wetting my clothes. I was about to cry when a dark shadow appeared in front of me. Miss Crow was standing there, staring down at me in her long black coat, looking angry.

Chapter 12
The Orphanage

"Hurry up!" I manage to walk to the car with great difficulty. She opens the car door, pushes me onto the back seat, and drives away. About an hour later, the car stops. She gets out, opens the back door, pulls me out by one arm, and drags me up a flight of stairs, repeating, "Walk properly, don't play up." I want to say, "I can hardly walk, I've only been a human girl a few days." She knocks at the front door, and we wait for a few minutes until it is opened by a portly man holding a large stick. He looks at me and says to Miss Crow, "Is this the child you want me to have for a few days?" She replies, "Yes, this is the child that was found in the Andersons' house. They knew nothing about her or how she got there."

"I hope she's toilet trained and behaves herself," he says, then introduces himself, saying, "I'm Mr. Cross. Little girl, how old are you?" I try to answer, but a mixture of sounds comes out. Then he asks Miss Crow to follow him upstairs to the first floor with me, where he has a room ready for me to share with another girl. The orphanage is a gloomy place with three floors, and the whole place smells musty and damp. On reaching the first floor, we follow him down a corridor until we reach room twelve. He stops, opens the door, and ushers us into the room. It's dark green with two beds, a small cupboard, and nothing else apart from a small window, which is closed. He points to the bed that I'll be using and says, "Put your things in the cupboard."

Miss Crow stands watching me, irritated, as I make an attempt to pick up my bag but can't it's too heavy. She comes over, snatches the bag from me, and begins to unpack my things and put them in the cupboard. Once she's finished, she grabs me aggressively and puts me on the bed. She speaks to me, saying, "You're going to learn to talk quickly and stop your whimpering." I begin to cry, and she says, "Shut up, I'm sick of your crying." Mr. Cross points to the stick in his hand, adding, "If you're not good, you'll learn what this is quickly." He says, "When the bell rings, it's time to go downstairs for dinner." Were people going to treat me like this from now on? I was taken away from the Andersons, why couldn't I stay with them?

The room is really cold, so I get into bed to keep warm and fall asleep. I'm woken up by the sound of a bell ringing. I get out of bed, try to walk but can't, and the bell doesn't stop ringing. Confused, I sit back on the bed, not knowing what to do. Then the door opens, and a girl comes in. She is quite tall with long blond hair and a pretty face, about twelve years old, reminding me of Amanda. She looks at me with a puzzled expression and says, "You're going to be in trouble if you don't get downstairs in time for dinner. My name's Holly Parker. Can you walk?" I nod, get off the bed, make an attempt to walk, and fall over. She helps me up, takes me to the bathroom, washes my face, combs my hair, then picks me up and carries me downstairs to the dining room, and we go in for dinner.

Mr. Cross comes in as we sit down and makes his way to the end of the table to a large leather chair, says grace, and dinner begins. On my first night at dinner, it's a bowl of soup, mashed potatoes with mincemeat, prunes, and custard. Eating is new for me and hard to cope with, and Holly makes several attempts to feed me while Mr. Cross isn't looking. After dinner, some of the children go to watch TV or read until bedtime at 8:30 p.m. when the bell rings again for us to go up to our rooms. How was I going to climb those stairs without help? Once again, Holly comes to my rescue, throws her long cardigan over me, and carries me upstairs. On reaching our room, she puts me down on my bed and says, "Wasn't that fun?" reminding me of Amanda again.

Next, I make several attempts to put my pyjamas on but can't and fall over. My new friend helps me, then tucks me into bed.

44

"Goodnight, do you have a name?" I say, "Sal ye." "Oh, your name's Sally. Go to sleep now." I dream of Amanda again that night when I sleep, and she repeats, "Everything's going to be alright."

The following morning the bell rings at 6.30 a.m. Holly shouts to me, "Get up! We've got to get to the bathroom before the other kids do, to wash, then back here to dress. Breakfast is at 7 a.m. in the dining room. If you're late, you get the cane." I ask, "Why?" She replies, "You're too small to understand. It's called discipline, that's how it works here." Once we are ready, she carries me downstairs quickly to the dining room, and we arrive a few seconds before Mr. Cross comes in and takes his place at the table. He stands for a few seconds, checking to see if there are any empty places at the table and children missing, says grace, and breakfast begins. When it ends, the older children study for the next few hours, and I am taken to the office by one of the staff, as the placement service is coming that morning.

On reaching the office, Rebecca Crow is already there, sitting in a large armchair, wearing her usual clothes and pointed shoes. That morning her face seems even whiter, and her nose longer. On seeing me, she points to a chair, saying, "Sit on it." I walk over to the chair, make several attempts to climb onto it, and end up on the floor. She is furious, rushes over to me, grabs me off the floor, and puts me onto the chair with such force that it leaves me trembling in fear. Then, with a sudden movement, she gets hold of me and shakes me violently. I wet my knickers, and she screams, "I'll give you something to cry about," then slaps my legs non-stop!

While she is doing this, Mr. Cross comes into the room, stops her, and says, "Your aggressive temper with this small child could get the orphanage closed for cruelty to homeless children. I'm the only person who can apply punishment to any of the children here. Do I make myself clear?"

He then comes over to wipe my nose and tears with a handkerchief and rings for a care assistant to take me to wash my hands and face, as the Andersons are waiting for me in the lounge. As we leave the office, there is a quarrel going on between Mr. Cross and Miss Crow, with raised voices.

Chapter 13
Holly and the Andersons

Mrs. Anderson got up as I was brought into the lounge and said, "I've been worrying about you all night." She picked me up, and I put my arms around her neck and hugged her. Her husband joined us, held my hand, and said, "You've stolen our hearts, Gran's as well, and she'll be in to see you before she goes home." Then he left to talk with Mr. Cross. His wife put me on her lap, pressed the buzzer, and ordered a pot of tea and milk for me.

Mr. Anderson was gone for some time and seemed worried when he returned. His wife asked, "What's wrong?" He replied, "There's still no news of a missing child in our area. Mr. Cross has informed the police and given them a full description of Sally, but no one's come forward with any information." They were both silent, then he said, "That means Sally will have to remain here as a child with no identity until there's some information about who she is."

Mrs. Anderson held me tight and asked, "How can we help her?" He replied, "We'll have to wait and see what happens over the next few weeks." While they were talking, Mr. Cross came back into the room, heard what Mr. Anderson said, and replied, "I'll let you know if there's any progress. You're both welcome to visit your little friend whenever you want to." The bell rang for lunch. Mrs. Anderson took my hand and walked to the dining room with me, gave me a hug, and said, "We'll be back to see you soon, Sally," and they left.

After lunch, we went up to our room, and Holly started to tell me about her life before she came into the orphanage. She told me about her parents, who managed a successful business in Spain importing English clothes. As they travelled a lot for work, Holly was left in England with an aunt to continue her studies. During school holidays, she'd fly out to Spain to be with her parents. Then her parents changed their usual plans the previous Christmas and decided to spend it in England with Holly and her aunt. All the arrangements were made for them to come to England. On the day of the flight, on their way to the airport by car, her parents had a fatal accident, and her mother was killed. Her father survived the accident but was left badly injured, needing full-time care, which meant he couldn't look after Holly.

The aunt whom she'd been living with was being paid to take care of her. After her father's accident, he was unable to work and couldn't pay the full amount of money to the aunt to look after Holly, and she decided not to anymore. That's how she ended up in the orphanage. After telling me about her father, she began to cry and said, "I always go to visit him on Sundays." I copied Mrs. Anderson and gave her a hug. That was the beginning of our long friendship. Over the following weeks, I grew more confident as my walking improved, and Holly began to teach me how to pronounce words. "Who'd believe the transformation that I'd gone through to become a girl?"

A week after the Andersons' visit, a career came into the bedroom one afternoon to tell me that someone was waiting to see me downstairs. On reaching the lounge, I was surprised to find Gran sitting there. She got up as I came in, came over, picked me up, and gave me a hug, saying, "I've missed you. As I'm going home tomorrow, I came to see you before I leave." After climbing onto her lap, I told her about Holly, whom I shared a room with, who reminded me of Amanda. On mentioning her granddaughter's name, she was tearful and asked, "Is Holly real?" "She is, Gran." She said, "I'd like to meet her. Can you go and get her?" I replied, "I'll try to find her." I went to the dining room and found her there, putting plates out for lunch. "Gran wants to meet you, she's in the lounge." I   said.

On arrival in the lounge, there was a look of surprise on Gran's face when we walked in. I introduced her to Holly, and she remarked, "It's a sign from God." Holly had a cup of tea with her, told her a little bit about her life, then excused herself and returned to help in the dining room. I stayed with Gran until lunchtime when she got up to leave and said, "I'll be back to see you soon," kissed me, then left.

That evening after dinner, Mr. Cross told us to wait as he had something to tell us. There was a weird silence as we sat waiting to hear what he wanted to say. Were there going to be some new rules to keep, or was somebody going to be punished? After tapping his cane on the table, he said, "There's going to be an outing to Greendale Forest next week." After telling us about the trip, he brought his cane down on the table with a loud bang and said, "I won't tolerate any bad behaviour on the outing, and if any of you cause trouble, you'll be severely punished. Do you all understand?" Everyone was silent, and he dismissed us.

Once we were back in our room, we didn't stop talking about the outing, and Holly planned to take her camera with us to take some photos while we were in the forest. I'd never been on an outing and was looking forward to going when I drifted to sleep that night. I hadn't been asleep long when Amanda appeared to me in a dream and said, "Be careful on the outing." After the dream, I was unable to sleep. I didn't mention anything about the dream to Holly during that week but felt anxious as preparations went ahead for the outing and kept thinking about Amanda's warning about something unexpected happening to us on the outing.

Everyone helped to prepare the food that we were taking with us for the outing, and we also had snacks with us in case we were delayed on the journey. The trip to Greendale Forest turned out to be a memorable one that Holly and I will never forget.

Chapter 14
Greendale Forest

On the day of the outing, although I was excited, I kept thinking about Amanda's warning and the dream I had. After breakfast, Mr. Cross gave us one last reminder about behaving ourselves. He told us to gather everything we needed for the day and line up in the hall, ready to leave when the coach arrived. It came on time, we boarded, settled into our seats, and left for Greendale Forest. It was a long journey, and Holly took some photos while we were on the coach. Mr. Cross also took some group photos.

The outing was in autumn. It was sunny but cold, and you needed a coat or a thick jacket. I didn't have either and wore the cardigan Gran had given me. Holly brought a blanket from our room in case it got colder during the day. Upon our arrival at the forest, everyone helped set up the folding table and get the camping stove ready to heat up lunch. Once everything was ready, we gathered around the table. Mr. Cross said grace, and lunch began. After we finished eating, we were taken on a guided walk of the forest and given some information about its history. Mr. Cross pointed out some of the dangers hidden in the natural environment of the forest, mentioning that below the heavy undergrowth, there could be various deep holes laid to catch animals. That's why he insisted we stay together in groups and not wander off alone.

During the guided walk, I noticed the large skeletal branches of the trees everywhere in the forest, along with the pungent smell from the pine trees. When we reached the lake, it looked dark and foreboding. There was a large notice board next to it with a warning sign, "Deep and Dangerous." Mr. Cross told us to sit down on the grass and began to tell us some stories about people who had come to the forest on day trips or alone and had disappeared. Some of the missing people had been children who vanished without a trace. Despite searches of the forest, none of the missing people were ever found. After hearing his stories, I felt scared and squeezed Holly's hand. "There's nothing to be afraid of, I'm with you," she said. Beams of sunlight were shining through the trees while Mr. Cross was talking to us, but when he left to sit on the coach, the forest seemed to grow dark quickly.

We were given two hours to explore the forest and told to be back at the coach to leave by 5 pm. Holly took more photos by the lake, then we followed a group of children who went deeper into the forest, ambling along behind them for about an hour, before noticing they had disappeared. When we realized we were alone, the daylight was fading quickly, and it was getting colder. Being tired by then, we sat on a fallen tree trunk to rest and ate some sweets and a bit of cake left from lunch.

As we sat there, the daylight continued to fade, and night descended rapidly on the forest. Holly took hold of my hand, and we began to walk down a path we thought we had entered the forest by. After walking for some distance on the path, we realized we were lost and had taken the wrong one. It was darker and colder by then, so Holly took the blanket out of her backpack and wrapped it around me. We continued walking through the forest, hoping to find our way back to the lake and coach.

Suddenly, I tripped over something metal in the undergrowth and fell. A screeching sound came from where I lay on the ground. Holly grabbed me, and I clung to her, screaming. Then we were both falling in the darkness into a deep hole. As we reached the ground at the bottom, there was a loud crash as the metal lid of the trap closed over the hole. We were both in shock and didn't move, but lay where we had landed with a few cuts on our legs that were bleeding.

The hole we had fallen into was well hidden in undergrowth and deep, just as Mr. Cross had warned us about. It had been dug to trap animals, and we were caught in it, unable to get out as darkness fell on the forest.

Holly looked at her luminous watch in the dark and said, "It's nearly 5 pm. We're not going to get back to the coach in time to leave." I was panic-stricken, but she remained positive, repeating, "People will come to search for us, we'll be found." Being trapped underground is awful, with the noises of the forest around you and animals scurrying above the hole. The hours passed with no sounds of anyone coming to look for us. We hadn't eaten since lunchtime, were hungry, and ate the few biscuits Holly had in her backpack for emergencies. The forest was dark and cold by then. Holly covered me with the blanket, but I couldn't sleep, as I'm scared of the dark.

I lay awake, looking at the cover of the trap, and that's when I saw a greyish mist filtering through the metal wire of the trap. I was drowsy when I saw two beams of light shining through the darkness into the hole. Then, the face of a mystifying creature with pointed ears appeared, crouched over the metal cover of the trap, staring at me. There was nowhere to run, we were trapped in the hole and scared stiff. The creature was large, with long black hair streaked with silver. With a sudden movement, he bent lower over the trap cover, and I saw his large luminous eyes as he looked inside the hole.

"Is he going to rip the cover off the trap, attack us, and then eat both of us?" Holly woke up and looked directly at the creature, who stared back at her. She remarked, "The creature looks like a werewolf, maybe they do exist." I was frightened and about to wet my knickers when she said, "Hasn't this trip been an adventure we'll never forget?" She was so like Amanda, enjoying the scary experience.

The werewolf remained watching us and didn't move until he opened his mouth and howled, showing his enormous pointed teeth. A few seconds later, various other animals of the forest joined in, making strange, weird noises. "How could we sleep with all this going on?" The creature didn't rip the lid off the trap but sat there keeping watch. We were both tired and eventually drifted off into a troubled sleep. I woke up with a start and heard Amanda's voice say, "Don't be afraid, I'm here to tell you help is on the way. You'll be found soon."

My fear of the werewolf diminished as I watched him lying on the metal cover above us throughout the night, keeping watch with the other animals of the forest, guarding us. The darkness gradually lifted as the dawn of another day began, with us still in the trap. As daylight came, the werewolf was still lying on the metal lid until he got up and stretched. Then he crouched down again to take a last look at us and put his paw through a metal slit of the trap to say goodbye. Holly touched his paw, and a tear fell through the open slit of the trap. He stretched again, got up, and within seconds vanished into the heavy undergrowth of the forest.

A few minutes later, we heard people talking close to where we were and the sound of dogs barking, which gradually grew louder. We stood up together and began to shout as loud as we could, "We're over here, caught in a trap in the ground." The sound of barking dogs grew louder until we saw them looking through the trap cover with a policeman and Mr. Cross. "Thank God we've found the girls," Mr. Cross said. The rescue team worked quickly, and we were taken out of the trap. Mr. Cross picked me up, and a policeman helped Holly to a waiting ambulance by the lake, where we were both checked for injuries and then driven back to the orphanage by Mr. Cross. Upon our arrival, we were given something to eat and helped upstairs to our room.

Chapter 15
The Fight

The following day after breakfast, we were taken to the office to explain the accident in the forest. I was surprised to find the Andersons waiting there for me. Mrs. Anderson got up when she saw me, came over, kissed me, and said, "We've been worried since Mr. Cross phoned to tell us that you were both missing in the forest." Miss Crow was in the office and viewed me with an air of contempt from across the room. Then the door opened, and Mr. Cross came in and sat at his desk. He pointed his cane at Holly and asked her to explain what had happened in the forest. She gave him a detailed account of what took place, and he listened attentively to everything she said, appearing satisfied with her story.

Mr. Cross then asked her to leave as he wanted to talk with Mr. Anderson, who began the conversation by asking if there was any news about me yet. Mr. Cross replied, "There still isn't any news about who Sally is." Mrs. Anderson asked, "If nobody comes up with any information about her, can we start the procedure to adopt her?" Mr. Cross answered, "Yes, but it will take some time." After hearing that, she rushed over, picked me up, and began to cry. Mr. Cross gave me a wink, saying, "You'll be having regular visitors now, Sally." Mrs. Anderson added, "From Gran as well. We have to go now, dear, but we'll be back soon to see you." Before they left, she sat me on a chair next to Miss Crow, who smiled at me through clenched teeth.

Mr. Cross looked at Miss Crow before he left the office, saying, "I'll only be a few minutes," as he closed the door. She remarked, "So you've found yourself a home, you spoiled little brat." I was afraid of her and thought she might hit me again while no one was in the office. When the door opened, Mr. Cross came back into the office, spoke to Miss Crow, and said, "Sally will be staying here until there's some information about her," mentioning that the Andersons were interested in adopting me. After telling her, she looked at me and got up to leave, saying, "I'll pass that information onto the children's placement services," and left. Mr. Cross rang the bell, and a career arrived to take me to the dining room.

Holly was quiet throughout lunch that day. I asked, "What's wrong?" She replied, "I'm having some trouble with Oscar. He's trying to pick a fight with me." The kids in the orphanage were all frightened of him, he was a bully. She continued speaking, "He punched me in the dining room. I hit him back, and now things are going to get worse." After lunch, we went up to our room, and I told her the Andersons wanted to adopt me. She said, "That's great! You'll have parents and a home."

For the rest of the afternoon, I couldn't stop thinking about her problem with Oscar and said, "If there's a fight, I'll help you. I'll kick him non-stop." She burst out laughing and said, "What if you end up falling over and getting hurt?" I replied, "I'll have to get up and start punching him again." She responded, "I don't want you involved, Sally." Oscar had been spreading rumours that he wanted Holly's camera, which was a present from her father, and boasting that he'd fight her to get it. The fight took place a few days after our conversation about Oscar.

That day after lunch, Holly asked me to go up to the room and stay there as she had to talk to someone in the garden and would be up later. I went upstairs to our room, sat on the bed, and practiced my reading. Then tried to have a nap but couldn't sleep. There was still no sign of Holly. So, I decided to go downstairs to see where she was. On reaching the ground floor, I went through the kitchen door that led to the garden and saw a large crowd of kids watching a fight. I pushed my way through the crowd to the front and had a shock when I saw Oscar hitting and punching Holly repeatedly in the head.

I was terrified but had to do something to stop him. Holly suddenly lost her balance, fell backward onto the ground, and lay still. Oscar's attack on her grew more violent as he kicked her non-stop while she lay motionless. Overwhelmed with fear, I watched him and found an unknown strength to stop his aggressive attack on her. I ran straight at him and kicked him as hard as I could to stop him from hurting her. "Wham, bam! Pow!" I kicked him anywhere I could reach, non-stop, until he aimed his fist at my face. I ducked, and he missed punching me! Holly opened her eyes, saw me, tried to get up, and collapsed back onto the ground with her head bleeding.

Next, I ran across the garden with Oscar following me in a raging temper. I saw a garden rake propped up against the wall, managed to grab it before he reached me, and as he came towards me, I hit him with it. He lost his balance, toppled over, and fell backward onto the patio, lying still. The kids who were watching the fight cheered, shouting, "Good on you, squirt, you've done it." I didn't move but stood holding the rake over him to make sure he didn't get up.

While I was standing near Oscar, holding the rake, Mr. Cross came into the garden to see what was going on and break it up. He saw me with the rake and Oscar lying on the ground. He started to laugh and said, "What's been going on? Have you been fighting with this big boy, Sally?" After Mr. Cross arrived, an ambulance was sent for, and Holly was taken to the hospital. She spent a week there before returning to the orphanage. Oscar was lifted to his feet by two of the staff and sent to the hospital as well.

After the fight, Mr. Cross wanted Oscar transferred to another home quickly, as his vicious attack on Holly was a sign of what he could do to other children. When Holly returned to the orphanage after being in the hospital, she had to take things easy and never complained about her injuries when the nurse came to visit her over the following weeks. After the fight, many changes took place. Mr.

Cross walked around more often, and there were always staff in the garden whenever any of the kids were out there playing. The news of the fight got back to the Andersons, who worried about Holly's injuries and her being in the hospital. They planned to have me adopted by Christmas and living with them. During that winter, the home filled out a form with information that I was four years old, able to walk, talk, and was toilet trained. Mr. Cross mentioned that no one had come forward with any information and said, "The Andersons are applying to adopt me."

I knew no one would come forward with any information about me. "How could they? Only I knew the truth that I'd been Amanda's doll, transformed into a girl. Who would believe that story?" So, my transformation remained a secret.

Chapter 16
December in the Orphanage

Mr. Cross was kept busy during December, arranging the Christmas Day lunch for relatives who were coming to visit the kids in the orphanage. He also oversaw all the events taking place during the festive season, which included forming a choir to sing in the town square and rehearsing a nativity play to be performed in the church. On the Saturday before Christmas, I was surprised by a visit from Gran, who arrived by minicab to see me. I knew she was spending Christmas with the Andersons and hadn't expected to see her until then.

When I got to the lounge, she was sitting on the couch surrounded by lots of bags and got up as I came in to kiss me, saying, "The weather's freezing cold, it's snowing again, so I went shopping to buy you a warm coat and boots." Then she asked, "How's everything going here? I hope Holly's getting better?" Gran didn't like Miss Crow and gave me her opinion of her, saying, "I've done nothing but worry about you since that woman put you here. I just don't like her." I said, "I don't either." She continued talking and said that her son had kept her updated with our news when he phoned her, and they were worried about me being in the home until my adoption papers were completed.

Gran looked tired, yawned, and said she was starving. She asked, "Can I get a cup of tea and something to eat? I'm famished, I haven't eaten since breakfast." Mr. Cross came into the lounge while she was saying this, and got the staff to get her some sandwiches and tea. Once she'd finished eating, Gran wanted to open the bags of presents she'd bought for me. She began with the largest bag, which contained a royal blue coat and hat. The next bag had a pair of red boots and patent leather shoes. The other bags had a variety of things, including pyjamas, jumpers, skirts, trousers, and the last bag had a beautiful pink party dress. I said, "Wow!" as she took it out of the bag. "I'd never had so many things given to me," I thanked Gran. She hugged me, sat me on her lap, and stayed for a couple of hours. She left by minicab later that afternoon for the Andersons' house, where she was staying that weekend.

The next day, it didn't stop snowing, and the garden of the orphanage was covered with deep snow. At breakfast, Mr. Cross said we could go outside to build a snowman. So, once breakfast ended, everyone rushed outside into the garden. We built a snowman, with everyone helping to put him together. He looked fantastic once he was finished, and we hoped he wouldn't melt for a couple of days. The days leading up to Christmas passed quickly with choir practice and rehearsals for the nativity play, so we were kept busy with the events going on up to Christmas.

One afternoon, Mr. Cross asked us to sort out the Christmas decorations for the tree. When we'd finished doing that, we went up to our room for a rest as we had to go back down later that afternoon to do some more jobs. On arrival upstairs, we found the door of our room open and Cora O'Connor in our bedroom, standing by the cupboard holding Holly's camera, about to steal it. As we came into the room, she hid the camera behind her back, and Holly said, "Put the camera down on the bed and leave." Cora didn't respond and kept it behind her back. So, I shouted, "Give Holly her camera back." She was fuming, came over, hit me across the face, and pushed me. I grabbed her hair to stop myself from falling and didn't let go, and we ended up on the floor fighting, with me screaming non-stop.

One of the staff heard me, came running into our room, saw what was going on, and rang the alarm bell! Mr. Cross arrived quickly, separated us, and said, "Stop screaming." He looked at Cora and knew what she'd been up to, as she was still holding the camera. After taking it from her, he handed it to Holly, told Cora to go to the office and wait for him there. He told us to go downstairs, get a drink, come back to our room, and stay there until lunchtime. Holly was traumatized by the incident as she hadn't fully recovered from the fight and being in hospital.

The Andersons had already made arrangements with Mr. Cross for us both to spend Christmas with them, and Holly was joining us after visiting her father on Christmas morning. We were looking forward to the events during the festive season. The Andersons came for one more visit before we went to stay with them and seemed happy about the progress they were making with my adoption formalities. Mrs. Anderson said, "You could be living with us by the New Year, as our daughter." I could see Holly reminded the Andersons of their daughter Amanda, and was glad she was spending the Christmas break with me.

Throughout time, I thought Amanda's ghost was behind the plan for me to be adopted by her parents to continue the friendship we had when I was her doll. We had so many adventures together when she'd taken me up to the attic with her, which was now kept locked. Maybe one day, I'd find out for myself if the manifestations were still happening in the attic. Holly was resting on her bed when the bell rang for lunch. She got up quickly, combed her hair, and said, "Let's go down for lunch, Sally."

On arrival downstairs, after seating ourselves at the dining table, Cora gave me a hard kick under the table. I knew it was her and yelled, "You pig!" Mr. Cross heard me and asked, "Who are you yelling at?" I pointed at Cora. He guessed she'd kicked me as she was sitting opposite, pointed to her with his cane, and said, "Go to the office." Oscar heard him, jumped up from where he was sitting at the table, and was heading towards me, waving his fist. Two of the staff restrained him and led him away to the office. Holly looked at me, started to laugh, which she hadn't done for a long time, and said, "You're my hero." I copied Mr. Cross and gave her a thumbs up.

We had choir practice that afternoon. I couldn't sing in tune, and my singing got worse with each carol we sang until I sounded like a cat when you tread on its tail. The other kids tried not to laugh as I was the youngest and smallest member of the choir. During choir practice, I was given a stool to stand on, which I kept falling off. When this happened, there'd be roars of laughter from the other kids. Mr. Cross would look at me and say, "You at it again, Sally?"

A couple of days before Christmas, a large tree was delivered and put in the lounge. We were given a variety of different decorations and told to decorate the tree the following afternoon. Holly was given some fairy lights, and I had some angels to hang on the tree. That night, when I went to bed and slept, I heard Amanda's voice say, "Soon we will be together, and I'll be waiting for you in the attic." I woke up puzzled by what she said.

The Andersons came to visit on Sunday and brought presents for us. We spent the afternoon with them. Holly was tearful when she was given her presents. Mrs. Anderson gave her a hug, saying, "You're both part of our family now. I'm looking forward to having you both with us for Christmas." They left late that afternoon.

The orphanage was dimly lit that evening as we made our way upstairs, then through the corridor that led to our room. On reaching our room, a misty apparition of a figure about Holly's height appeared in front of the door for a few seconds, then faded and vanished. Holly remarked, "This place is haunted, and a ghost seems to be following us." That night, I couldn't sleep, but Holly slept quickly like a log.

The following day after lunch, we went to the lounge to decorate the Christmas tree. Holly was standing on the ladder putting the fairy lights around the tree when the door opened. Guess who came in? Yes, it was Cora, who came running into the room being chased by Oscar. They ran straight into the ladder, knocked it at an angle, with Holly clinging onto the tree. The tree flew across the room and ended up on the floor with a crash! That left Holly lying on the floor with the tree on top of her.

The noise brought staff quickly to the lounge. Mr. Cross arrived with some of the staff who helped Holly up from where she was lying on the floor. Mr. Cross was angrier this time with Cora and Oscar for causing more trouble and another accident. Oscar was in a vicious temper, clenched his fist to punch Mr. Cross, and was restrained by staff, then taken out of the room to the office. I attempted to hit Cora and was handed over to a career.

There was an overwhelming silence when they left, broken a few minutes later by screaming and shouting coming from the office. The front doorbell rang, and an ambulance arrived to take Holly to the hospital for a check-up. She was quite pale when they left, and I wasn't allowed to go with her. She returned later that evening and was helped upstairs to our room, where she remained for the next couple of days. During that time, the Andersons came to visit again and brought some goodies to cheer her up and a toy for me. Mrs. Anderson kept me on her lap for the whole visit and repeated, "It won't be long, you'll be at home with us soon and safe."

She also reassured Holly that she'd always be welcome to stay with them at any time. Having the Anderson family in our lives had made a great difference, showing us, they cared and accepted us into their family. Over the following days, some of the kids came to get me for choir practice while Holly was confined to our room. It was

Christmas Eve, and it hadn't stopped snowing all day, settling in the garden quite deep.

I remember that Christmas well, going into the lounge with Holly where a log fire was burning, and the sound of carols being sung on the radio. Mr. Cross ended up putting the fairy lights on the tree himself, and they looked magical. It was my first Christmas as a girl, and I loved every moment of it, excited about being adopted soon by the Andersons.

Chapter 17
Christmas Events

It was still snowing when the coach arrived to take us into the town centre, where our choir was singing that afternoon for charity. Holly and I were wrapped up in duffle coats, gloves, and boots as we boarded the coach. It was going to be a busy day with lots going on, including a party. The Andersons were also coming to get me later that evening to spend Christmas and the New Year with them. Since my transformation, so many things had changed for me, and my secret was kept well-hidden being Amanda's doll. Once my adoption papers were completed, her parents would be mine, and I'd be their daughter, living in the house where Amanda grew up, with a new identity and life.

When we reached the town centre and left the coach, there was a large crowd of people waiting to hear us sing. Mr. Cross looked grand as he got off the coach, wearing a black cape, a large-brimmed hat, and carrying a walking stick. A few minutes later, we formed a half-circle, ready to begin singing carols. Mr. Cross waved his stick in the air, and we began to sing a medley of carols. We started with "Oh Little Town of Bethlehem," which the public generously applauded. Then I was given a stool to stand on for the next carol, "The Little Drummer Boy." During that carol, my singing got worse, I sneezed, wiped my nose, and fell off the stool. Holly helped me up and back onto the stool, while the public roared with laughter and clapped. Mr. Cross smiled and gave me a thumb-up once we'd finished singing. Then we were ushered into the church hall for a party and given a present each to unwrap on Christmas Day.

It snowed for the whole journey back to the orphanage, and I wondered if the Andersons would come to collect me that evening. Upon arrival, we were taken into the lounge, where a fire was burning brightly. A large table was laid out with mince pies and a variety of cakes. The Christmas tree was covered with decorations and fairy lights in different colours that twinkled. The whole room looked fantastic, with lots of presents placed around the base of the tree. I said, "Wow! I've never seen anything like this before. It's magical." Then one of the staff told us there was hot chocolate being served in the kitchen, with sandwiches, mince pies, fruit, and sweets in the lounge.

While we were eating, I looked at the clock and asked Holly, "What's the time?" She replied, "Nearly 7:30. I hope the Andersons are okay driving here to get you, as it hasn't stopped snowing." After she said that, the phone rang in the hall. We looked at each other, anticipating bad news, thinking there might have been an accident. Mr. Cross answered the call and came into the room to tell me that the Andersons were on their way but would be late due to heavy traffic and snow. We felt relieved, and Holly said, "They're just going to be late. Let's go and get another mince pie." We stayed downstairs all evening, but felt anxious until they arrived to get me.

Mr. Cross came back into the room to wish us all a Happy Christmas and told us to go up to our rooms. We followed the other kids upstairs in semi-darkness. On reaching the corridor where our room was, there was less light and a transparent ball of light floating near us until we reached the door of our room, where it vanished. As Holly opened the door of our room, she remarked, "We've got a ghost following us, haven't we?" I replied, "I think so. It scares me."

We were about to get ready for bed when a member of staff came into our room and said, "Remain dressed, Sally. The Andersons have arrived and are downstairs." Holly grinned, saying, "It's all going to work out. Get your coat, and I'll get your bag." After doing that, we made our way downstairs and found the Andersons standing in the hall looking tired and covered in snow.

Mr. Cross showed them into the lounge to have something to eat and drink before they left with me for the return journey home. Holly kissed them both, and Mrs. Anderson said, "We'll be waiting to see you after you visit your father on Christmas Day." She gave me a hug, then went up to bed. My future mum picked me up and put me on her lap while she drank her tea, then carried me outside to the car, put me in a sleeping bag, and laid me on the back seat of the car to sleep. The journey back to the Andersons' home was a long one. Mum woke me several times to see if I needed to use the toilet.

On arrival home, we went into the kitchen, where Gran was dozing in a chair and woke up as we entered. She came over to give me a hug, then began to cook breakfast for everyone. While we were eating, a misty image of Amanda appeared near the kitchen door that was open. But wasn't she dead? Once we'd finished eating, Gran picked me up, carried me upstairs, and said, "It's time for bed. Father Christmas is due tonight, and you must be asleep before he comes." She helped me into pyjamas, tucked me into bed, said, "Night, night, sleep well," kissed me, and left the night light on.

On Christmas Day, I woke up early and found a large stocking filled with toys, presents, and a large brown teddy bear at the end of my bed. Inside the stocking, there were lots of toys to play with, hair slides, ribbons, and a pair of slippers. Gran's room was next door to mine, so I went to tell her what Father Christmas had brought me. When I knocked on her bedroom door, she opened it and asked, "Did Father Christmas come? What did he bring you?" Then she sat me on her bed, and I told her what I'd found in my Christmas stocking. She listened and said, "Go put your slippers on, and we'll go down to have breakfast together." After putting my slippers on, we went downstairs to the kitchen.

During breakfast, I felt that we were being watched the whole time we were in the kitchen. Then a draft blew through the kitchen that slammed the door shut. Gran jumped with a start and said, "There must be a window open somewhere in the house causing these drafts." After the door shut, my new parents, the Andersons, arrived for breakfast, looking happier that Christmas morning. Dad turned the TV on, and Mrs. Anderson came over to me, picked me up, and sat me on a chair next to her. She said, "Sally, why don't you start calling us Mum and Dad? Soon you'll be living here with us as our daughter." Her husband looked at her, agreeing with a wink.

Dad asked, "What did Father Christmas bring you? I know you want to tell me." I got up from the table, took his hand, and led him upstairs to my room to show him everything I'd got. He picked up my teddy bear and asked, "Can I have him?" Gran had come upstairs with us. I looked at her and said, "No, he's mine." She looked at Dad and said, "You're both a pair of kids," gave Dad a slap on his bottom, and said to me, "It's time for your bath and to get dressed." After having a bath, Gran put the pink party dress on me and placed a bow in my hair. My first Christmas with the Andersons and Gran was the beginning of many happy memories that I treasure, being their daughter.

Recalling that Christmas, once I was dressed, Gran took me downstairs to the lounge. When she opened the door, I was surprised to see such a large Christmas tree. It was covered with glittering silver lights shaped like stars, and baubles in different colours glittered all over the tree. At the top of the tree, there was a fairy doll dressed in white, wearing a crown made of silver star dust. "Wow! She's lovely, glittering with stars all around her." Gran put me on the couch, sat next to me, and took some chocolates out of her apron pocket. She said, "It's a secret, as we're not supposed to eat anything until lunchtime," grinned, and popped another chocolate in her mouth, giving me one. I gobbled mine up quickly and kissed her. I loved Gran, as she reminded me of Amanda.

Holly arrived just before lunch by minicab, and Mrs. Anderson took her upstairs to my room that we were sharing. I went with them to have a chat with her before lunch. As Mum left us, she said, "Unpack quickly, then come down for dinner." Holly seemed sad after visiting her father, as his health wasn't improving, so she'd have to remain in the orphanage until his situation changed. While we were chatting, Gran came into the bedroom to tell us that lunch was going to be served, and we followed her downstairs to the lounge.

The table looked Christmassy with lots of decorations, and there were flowers everywhere around the room, with lots of candles placed around the room and on the Victorian fireplace. I sat between Holly and Gran for Christmas dinner. My future Mum and Dad sat opposite us. Once everyone was seated at the table, Dad carved the turkey, said grace, and dinner began. I tried all the different dishes of food at Christmas dinner, and Gran winked at me, saying, "You're just like me, Sally," as I ate another roast potato. Mum got up, left for the kitchen, and came back carrying a pudding that was on fire, saying, "That's what we're having next." I had some of it with cream. Holly looked at me and said, "Slow down, you'll be sick."

After lunch, there were more presents from under the tree, and Mum gave me a large doll dressed in a school uniform named Amanda, who looked like her. Holly got a jumper and handbag from Gran, which she liked. Mum gave her a voucher to buy what she needed. Everyone played board games while I sat watching and must have fallen asleep. Because when I woke up, I was covered with a blanket on the couch. Mum then suggested going for a walk to the heath to get some fresh air, and Holly helped me to get ready. Snowflakes were falling as we left the house, and the garden was covered with glittering white snow.

On reaching the heath, there were some squirrels scurrying around in the trees and a dog out for a walk, who came running over to us.

Dad took some photos of us, which I still have in my photo album. It continued snowing while we were at the heath and gradually became heavier as we walked back to the house. On arrival back, the snow surrounding the house had become deeper and shone in the twilight as we walked up the drive to the house. And I noticed a figure at the bedroom window again, watching us. Could it be Amanda's ghost?

We had afternoon tea in the lounge on arrival home and spent the rest of the evening playing games and watching TV. That Christmas Day, I felt happy with my new life and about being the Andersons' daughter soon. Which meant I'd have a life like Amanda had before her death, who seemed to haunt me more since my arrival back in the house. Her presence seemed to be everywhere I went, as though she was watching me. That night, as we got ready for bed, Holly mentioned how much she enjoyed being with the family and was looking forward to the rest of the holiday with them. So, I didn't mention anything about what I was experiencing since I'd returned to the house.

Chapter 18
Boxing Day

On Boxing Day, Gran came into our room to get us up, saying, "Breakfast is in an hour," then helped me shower and dress. Holly got ready quickly and came downstairs with us. Mum was already in the kitchen when we arrived, cooking breakfast, and Gran went to help her. During breakfast, Mr. Anderson mentioned that since it had stopped snowing, we could go for a drive to Grange Wood Park, where they had winter activities and toboggans for hire by the hour, which might be fun. He asked, "Are you interested in going to the park?" We both said, "Yes, we'd love to go." He replied, "Okay, go put your coats on, boots, hats, and hurry up. Don't forget gloves." We dashed off upstairs and came back down in a few minutes.

Mum was already in the hall waiting when we got there, dressed in a white furry coat with a hood and wearing boots. Dad was standing next to her, dressed in a heavy dark coat with a Russian-style hat, waiting for Gran. She came downstairs a few minutes later, dressed in a bright red anorak, spotted boots, and a Christmassy hat with a bobble. She grinned, saying, "If I get lost, you'll be able to find me quickly." Dad handed Mum the car keys and said, "Make your way to the car. I have to check the back door before we leave."

It was a cold, blustery day as we made our way to the car. Before getting into it, I looked up at the bedroom window. The curtains moved, and a misty figure stared down at us. Who was it? Once we were in the car, I whispered to Holly what I'd seen. She replied, "It was probably the wind blowing the curtain that caused the shadowy image." I insisted, "It wasn't. I felt it might be Amanda trying to show me that she was in the house."

It was a short drive to Grange Wood Park, and we spent a great afternoon there. Dad hired a couple of sledges, and we took turns riding them. Gran had a couple of rides with me, nearly lost her hat, enjoyed herself, and kept saying during the ride, "I'm scared but loving it, go faster." Mr. Anderson stood watching her anxiously and shouted, "You've had enough rides, Mum, come off," with a worried expression. It was great fun at the park, and we left late in the afternoon to drive back home.

Dad parked the car in the driveway upon arrival home. As we got out of the car, I shivered and took Gran's hand as we walked towards the house, which looked large and mysterious against the evening sky, with deep snow around it. We'd had a good afternoon at the park, and the evening lay ahead to enjoy. Both women went to the kitchen straight away to fix something to eat, and we headed for the lounge to watch "White Christmas," which was showing on TV. When it ended, the food was ready, and we sat eating while watching a variety show. Later that evening, my parents played cards, and we played a game of Snap until bedtime. We said goodnight to everyone and then followed Gran upstairs to our bedroom, which was next to hers.

We were tired that night. Holly helped me get into my pyjamas. We didn't chat but went straight to bed and fell asleep quickly. During the night, I woke up suddenly, shivering, and felt that someone was in the room watching me. I saw a faint mist in one of the corners of the room, similar to what I'd seen with Amanda in the attic. Scared and shivering, I put the duvet cover over my head, not wanting to wake Holly, who was asleep in the other bed. I must have fallen asleep again, as the next thing I heard was Gran's voice saying, "Get up, girls, it's time to get ready and come down for breakfast," and she left to start cooking.

After showering and dressing quickly, we went down to the kitchen. On arrival, we found Gran singing to pop music blaring from the radio. She stopped singing upon our arrival and said, "Start putting plates out for breakfast." While we were doing that, the Andersons came in and sat down at the table, and Gran dished up a full English breakfast. Once we had finished eating, Dad said, "I've got some work to catch up on today and will be in the basement." Mum added, "I'm going into town with Gran to the supermarket for some shopping." That meant we were alone for a couple of hours and free to do what we wanted. Mum suggested that we take a walk around the area where the house was to get to know it, or we could go into town with them. We decided to explore the area near the house, and it turned into another supernatural adventure.

Chapter 19
Langley Ewing's Haunted House

Since my arrival back at the house, all I'd wanted to do was go up to the attic and take Holly with me. I was about to ask her when she said, "Let's go for a short walk to get some fresh air." Gran heard her and said, "That's a good idea. Get your coats and take a walk, it'll do you both good." So, we went upstairs, got our coats, and as we were leaving, she hollered, "Enjoy your walk. Don't get lost. Lunch will be at 2 p.m. I'll be back by then."

After leaving the house, we walked straight down our road until we reached a crossroad. We took the road directly in front of us, which looked interesting and was lined with Victorian houses similar to the Andersons'. We continued walking down that road until we reached a large signpost with some information about a house called Rosamunde, which was in Collingdale Road. The house had been owned by a well-known artist in 1854, who'd painted many of the prominent people in that area. So, we continued walking until we reached the house, which had a large board standing next to the front door with "Langley Ewing's paintings on display" written on it. There was no entrance fee.

Holly looked at me and said, "Let's go in and have a look at the artist's work. We've got plenty of time." The door of the house was slightly ajar and seemed to be inviting us in. I took Holly's hand, and we went in to have a look at the paintings. While we were standing in the hall, a lady dressed in Victorian costume appeared out of nowhere and offered to show us around the house and give us some information about Langley Ewing's life and paintings. The woman spoke with a soft, clear voice and seemed accustomed to showing visitors around the house.

But there was something puzzling about the way she'd appeared in the hall without us seeing her arrive, and also about the clothes she wore. Holly said, "Her clothes are a gimmick she uses for visitors to create the atmosphere from that period."

The woman showing us the house and talking about Langley Ewing always walked slightly in front of us. That's when I noticed something out of the ordinary about her as we made our way upstairs. It was really odd because she wasn't walking on the stairs but seemed to float up them in front of us. On reaching the landing, I was walking behind her and could see that she wasn't on the floor but a few inches above it. I couldn't take my eyes off the strange phenomenon I was seeing.

Another surprise came when she stopped in front of Langley Ewing's portrait to explain that she was his granddaughter, who'd inherited the house along with his paintings after his death. On hearing that, we knew this was another paranormal adventure we were experiencing once we entered the house. After seeing the artist's painting of himself, I knew that he'd painted the portrait of Brigadier Anderson that was in the attic. Next, she asked us to follow her down a long corridor where she opened a door that led into a large drawing room decorated in Victorian style. She told us to sit on a sofa and began to tell us more about the artist's life and work.

There were several paintings hung on the walls of this room, lifelike images of the people in them, who seemed to be looking down at us from the walls of the room. Once she finished showing us around the house, we thanked her and were making our way downstairs to leave when I saw a large painting of a man in military uniform on the wall above the staircase. Holly asked, "Who's that man in military uniform?" The woman replied, "Oh, that's Brigadier Anderson, who used to live in this area. I was going to marry him if he hadn't been killed in the Crimean War."

"He lived in a large house called Whispering Echoes. People say that he haunts the place where he lived." I nudged Holly, saying, "That's where we're staying the Andersons' house." The woman ghost showing us the house said, "You might like to visit Whispering Echoes while you're in the area. It's not far from here." We stood looking at the portrait of the brigadier for a few moments. His image moved, and he winked.

The ghostly lady who'd been showing us the house came to the front door with us, stood by the open door to watch us leave, lifted her hand, waved us goodbye, then vanished, and the door closed slowly. We stood outside the house for a few seconds, baffled by what we'd just seen. Holly grabbed my hand, and we hurried away from Rosamunde House with its ghosts from the past that haunted it.

On arrival back at the Andersons' house, I wondered how many more ghosts lay hidden in the attic, waiting to haunt us. Our stay with the Andersons was coming to an end, with only a few days left before we were leaving. I'd grown used to being with the family, Holly had too, and loved spending time with Gran. We both didn't want to leave. Most days, the Andersons were both out at work, and Mum would phone a few times during the day to make sure that we were both okay, which made us feel secure, being part of their family. The prospect of leaving them made us both miserable. Although I knew that I'd be living with them very soon as their daughter, what was going to happen to Holly?

Chapter 20
Terrorized by Birds

A couple of days before we left to return to the orphanage, I told Holly about what I'd seen in the attic with Amanda when we ventured up there. She replied, "Do you want to go through another frightening experience?" I said, "There's some really strange paranormal stuff up there. We both saw the lady in grey vanish in front of us at Langley Ewing's House." She still wasn't convinced about what we had seen and said, "Leave those types of things alone."

When the Andersons returned home from work that evening, it was snowing and cold. Gran had been in her room most of the afternoon resting, and she came down before the Andersons returned to fix dinner. During the meal, Gran mentioned that she'd heard noises coming from the attic that afternoon and said, "I think there are rats up there." Mr. Anderson replied, "Mum, I'll look into it at the weekend when I have time." Holly said to Gran, "Don't let it worry you. It's probably rats." Mr. Anderson repeated, "I'll deal with it at the weekend."

After speaking to her son, Gran seemed happier and said, "I bought something special for dessert," and left for the kitchen. She returned carrying a large box, from which she took out a chocolate cake and cut it up for dessert. After dinner, we went into the lounge to watch *The Christmas Carol* on TV for the rest of the evening. At bedtime, we said goodnight to everyone and were on our way upstairs when a strong gust of air swept past us, almost throwing us downstairs. Holly clung to me until the strange phenomenon was over.

On reaching our room, she was badly shaken by the supernatural event that had just taken place. The following morning, she spoke to Gran about what had happened to us on the way upstairs the previous night. Gran replied, "It's the windows. They all need repairing. The whole house is full of drafts," and began to cook eggs and bacon. During breakfast, the Andersons came into the kitchen in a hurry, had toast and tea quickly. Mum said she'd phone us during the day, both of them kissed us, and left quickly. Gran said, "I'm going to visit some friends this morning. I'll be back in time to fix lunch," gave us a hug each, and left.

We were alone now, with an eerie silence covering the house once everyone had gone. Holly was still sitting at the table, looking anxious, and said, "Let's get the dishes washed so Gran doesn't have to do them when she gets back," and went to wash the remaining things in the sink. She told me to get our coats as we were going for a walk in the garden. After getting our coats, I showed her where the front door key was kept in the hall and saw the attic key hanging next to it. I couldn't reach it, but she could. Holly looked at me and seemed to know what I was thinking, and said, "We can't go up there without the Andersons' permission." After saying that, she opened the front door, and I followed her into the garden.

It was cold that day, and everything looked dismal, including the trees without their leaves. Their branches, being empty, created a circle surrounding the house that looked like skeletons against the dull, wintry sky. It was spooky. Although the atmosphere was strangely peaceful as we ambled through the garden and damp fallen leaves, there was an old bench under an oak tree. We sat on it to chat for a while. The silence in the garden was then broken by the sound of a flock of squawking birds. We both looked up and saw large birds flapping their wings and flying towards us, getting dangerously close.

We got up quickly and ran across the garden towards the front door, with the birds following us, screeching. Next, there was a loud crashing noise that came from the bedroom shutters as they hit the wall of the house. A transparent image of a girl appeared, watching us from the window. I shivered as goose pimples covered my entire body. Holly looked terrified, turned pale, grabbed my hand, and dragged me along with her until we reached the front door. She was shaking badly by then and couldn't open the front door, but after several attempts, the door opened.

Once we were safely inside the house, we headed for the kitchen to get a drink and sat there, relieved to be indoors again. The house was strangely peaceful, and we thought we were safe until a vibrant tapping noise began coming from the kitchen windows. Holly pulled the blinds up, and several large black birds were pecking at the glass non-stop, trying to break it and get into the kitchen. She pulled the blinds down quickly, but the noise didn't stop. We left the kitchen for the lounge to get away from the nerve-racking sound of the birds pecking at the windows. It was creepy being on our own in the house. I wished Gran would come back soon.

The atmosphere was tense for the next few minutes until we heard the front door open, then Gran calling out, "Are my girls back?" I replied, "We're in here, Gran." She said, "Get yourselves into the kitchen. Let's get lunch going." Once we were in the kitchen, she asked, "Why are the blinds pulled down?" Holly then explained to her what happened in the garden. She replied, "Those birds better stop their nonsense, or they'll end up being roasted for dinner." Holly opened the blinds, and the birds were gone. Gran commented, "Those birds saw me coming and did a runner." We both started laughing, which took away the fear we'd experienced. Lunch didn't take long, and when it ended, we went into the lounge to watch TV. Gran sat in her favourite armchair and dropped off to sleep.

While she slept, we changed channels on TV and watched a documentary film about various places and houses that were haunted. While we were watching it, Holly said, "Is that what you're always talking about, Sally?" I nodded. "It's true. Amanda and I saw a lot of weird things in the attic." We watched the rest of the film, with Gran's snoring growing louder, which sent Holly into hysterical laughter. Gran woke up with a start and asked, "Have you both eaten?" Holly said, "Yes," as the documentary film ended, and Gran got up to make some tea. Holly still had doubts about anything supernatural and remarked, "Everything has a logical explanation."

That evening when the Andersons returned home from work, Dad asked, "How did your day go?" Holly then gave him a detailed account of what took place in the garden with the birds and a brief one about the image we saw at the bedroom window, and said, "Both incidents were frightening as the birds followed us to the house, then began pecking at the kitchen window. It was really scary." But she never mentioned anything about the supernatural documentary film we'd watched on TV.

Our holiday was coming to an end, and Gran was planning to take us to see a pantomime that she'd been raving about nonstop. I remained determined to take Holly up to the attic before we left to see if the supernatural manifestations were still going on up there, which I'd seen with Amanda.

Chapter 21
Holly and Sally in the Attic

I had the chance to take Holly up to the attic a couple of days later, when the Andersons left for work. That morning, we occupied ourselves watching TV until lunchtime, and during lunch, the opportunity came when Gran complained of a bad headache and said, "I'm going up to my room to rest for a couple of hours." Once she left the kitchen, I knew we had enough time to go up to the attic while she was resting. Holly sensed what I was thinking and remarked, "Do you want us to get into trouble?" I replied, "We're leaving soon and won't get another chance." After a brief silence, she asked, "Where's the key for the attic kept?" I answered, "I'll show you," and we left the kitchen for the hall.

An uncanny silence hung over the house as I showed her where the key was kept in the hall. She looked guilty after taking the key from its hook, took my hand, and we began to make our way upstairs to the attic. The stairs creaked with every step we took, growing louder as we reached the top, where the attic door faced us. Holly took the key out of her pocket, hesitated, then went over to the door. She put the key in the lock, and the door opened easily with a loud screeching sound.

After telling her where the lights were, we went in. She couldn't find them at first, stumbled around in the dark, and screamed as something touched her foot. I was standing next to her in the dark when she found the light switch and turned it on. Then a loud bang sounded as the attic door shut. Holly had left the door open in case we needed to leave in a hurry. Since my last visit to the attic with Amanda, I hadn't been up there. I noticed her suitcase lying on top of a trunk, with some of the things she had taken to college with her on that last fatal trip. It was hard to believe that she was dead and that I'd never see her again. An eerie atmosphere hung over the attic.

I shivered as a pungent smell of decay began to engulf me, emanating from damp cobwebs hanging down from the rafters. The whole place was cold and creepy. Holly was nervous and said, "Let's have a quick look around and then go back downstairs." We did that, starting in one of the corners, making our way around the attic. I accidentally touched some of the hanging cobwebs. They were slimy and moved slightly after I touched them.

On reaching the middle of the attic, I saw a portrait of Brigadier Anderson hanging on a wall through the greyish mist rising from the floor around us. I nudged Holly, pulling her toward the corner where the portrait hung. We stood gazing at it for a few moments, and then the portrait came to life. The brigadier spoke, saying, "Your curiosity has brought you up to the attic again, Sally." On hearing his voice, Holly turned pale and sat on the trunk. I said, "Don't be afraid; everything will be okay." He spoke again, saying, "Amanda's here in the attic with me since her death." I couldn't believe what he said and sat on the trunk next to Holly. I had dreamt of Amanda several times since her death and thought it was because I missed her. What he said frightened me that she was a ghost in the attic, which was hard to believe.

We were both sitting on the trunk when I saw the hanging cobwebs shape-shifting into human-like forms, moving toward us in the semi-darkness. Holly saw them too and said, "I can't stand any more of this, let's go," and we got up quickly to leave. A strange silence filled the attic for a few moments, then a whoosh of air swept through the attic, and a transparent image of Amanda materialized in front of us. She lifted her hand to stop us from leaving and said, "I've waited so long to see you both and was in the forest with you throughout your adventure. I'm glad you're here now." "Thanks, Amanda. This is Holly, my friend from the orphanage, who's on holiday with me." Amanda giggled, said, "Nice to meet you," and then was gone!

Holly was freaked out after seeing Amanda and with the whole experience of the attic. As we went toward the door to leave, we found it being blocked by the shape-shifters.

The situation was terrifying as more rats appeared and ran around on the floor. Holly screamed as one of them scurried across her feet and cried out, "I can't stand any more of this hideous place! I wish I'd never come up here with you. Is there another way out?" I replied, "There is, through a gap in one of the walls, but I don't know which wall." While she was speaking, something flew into my hair. I shouted, "Holly, help me get whatever is in my hair out!" She replied, "It's a bat." She took her shoe off and waved it about in the air, making noises to frighten the bat. When it finally came out of my hair it flew up into the rafters of the attic, where it hung upside down, I was in shock, shaking, while the shape-shifters slithered across the floor, getting closer. I went hysterical and screamed, "What can we do?" Help came with a swirling ball of gold light that swept through the attic at speed and stopped suddenly.

The mist parted, and Brigadier Anderson appeared surrounded by a gold light. A tall, upright man dressed in military uniform with a sword in his belt, who had seen many victories on the battlefield, stood fearlessly facing the shape-shifters, ghouls, and ghosts of the attic. Defiant as they continued moving toward us, he said in a powerful voice, "Get away from my kin. Be gone! I banish you from this house, it belongs to me." Holly was about to faint when he turned to her and said, "Always be brave, dear. Hide your fear, because that's what ghouls, ghosts, and evil spirits thrive on. Fear is a powerful weapon used to frighten people. Do you understand?" She nodded and seemed calmer.

Then he pointed his sword at the moving shapes, spoke to them again in a foreign language, shouting. They stopped moving and began to disintegrate into a greyish matter, then disappeared completely.

Astounded by what we'd seen, we turned to speak to the brigadier, but he had vanished with the mist and ghosts of the attic.

Something fell on the floor next to me. I looked down and saw Amanda's friendship bracelet lying there. Should I pick it up and keep it? Holly looked at me and said, "Yes." Before leaving the attic, we took one last look at the brigadier's portrait. Holly nudged me, saying, "Did you see that? He winked at us." I replied, "You must be imagining things." Giggling, we went towards the door, which was open.

Once we were out of the attic, we rushed downstairs to the kitchen and found Gran there, preparing the evening meal. She was standing by the stove when we arrived and asked, "Where have you both been this afternoon?" I hate lying to her, so I said, "It's a secret." She wasn't fooled and replied, "I heard some noises going on in the attic. Were you both up there?" Holly replied, "Yes, we were up there. I'm sorry. We should have asked for your permission." She said, "As you've told me the truth, let's keep it a secret between us and don't go up there again." After giving Gran a hug, we stayed in the kitchen helping her and returned the key to its hook in the hall. Nothing more was mentioned about our visit to the attic.

That evening, when the Andersons returned from work, they gave us each a present, as the following day was our last one with them, and we would be returning to the orphanage. On the last day of our Christmas holiday, Gran took us to see the pantomime she had been raving about. It was fun. Afterward, we went for a fish and chip supper before returning home. Our Christmas holiday with the Andersons had been great, and I was looking forward to being adopted and living with them permanently. On our last night, Mum and Gran came upstairs with us at bedtime to help pack our things as we were leaving the following day after breakfast. Once everything was packed, we went downstairs for hot chocolate with Gran before going to bed. On reaching the kitchen, another gust of cold air whizzed past us. Gran remarked, "It's those upstairs windows; they need repairing. The whole house is full of drafts." When we finally got to bed that night, I dreamt of Amanda again. She spoke, saying, "Soon you'll be here for good, and I'm pleased that my plan is working out." I woke up after the dream, and the room was freezing cold. Our Christmas break was nearly over, together with the adventures we had, which Amanda would have loved, and now she was a part of herself.

Chapter 22
Returning to the Orphanage

Gran came into the bedroom early on the morning we were leaving, looking sad. She said, "It's time to get up, girls. I want you both to have breakfast before you leave." We got up quickly and went through our usual routine while Gran sat on the bed waiting for us. Once we were ready, we followed her downstairs to the kitchen. Holly laid the table while Gran cooked breakfast.

While she was doing this, the Andersons came into the kitchen and sat at the table. They were both quiet that morning at breakfast. My future mum got up suddenly, came over, gave me a hug, and said, "It won't be long, Sally, before you'll be here with us for good." Then she spoke to Holly, saying, "I want you to know that you'll always be welcome to come and stay with us," and was tearful. Mr. Anderson came over to his wife, put an arm around her, and said, "We've both enjoyed having you both with us for Christmas. Let's hope we can do this again this year." Gran was hugging Holly and crying, and said, "I'm going to miss both of my girls."

After breakfast, it was time to bring our bags down from the room to put in the car. While we were doing this, I had a feeling that we were being watched again. As we reached the bedroom door, we both saw a transparent apparition on the landing, which vanished within seconds. Was it Amanda? After getting our luggage from the room, we made our way downstairs to the hall, where everyone was waiting. Gran gave us another present each, kissed us both, and came outside to the car with us. Mr. Anderson put our luggage into the boot of the car and told us to get in.

Before getting into the car, I looked up at the bedroom window, and the ghostly figure was there, watching us. These manifestations we kept seeing were scary. I got into the car quickly and slammed the door shut. The drive back to the orphanage was a long one, and we stopped on the way for snacks.

On arrival back at the orphanage, Mr. Anderson rang the front doorbell and waited for a short time until Mr. Cross opened the door and took us into the lounge. He asked, "How was your Christmas?" We both replied, "It was great," and he said, "Go up to your room and unpack your things. I have to talk with the Andersons." We said goodbye to them. Mum said, "We'll be in to see you both on Sunday," and left.

Going back to our room after being with the family for Christmas was strange. After unpacking our bags, we sat talking about all the adventures we'd had during our Christmas break with the Andersons until the bell rang for dinner. We then went downstairs to join the other kids, who were already seated around the table in the dining room. After dinner, we watched TV for a short time and then were given the schedule for the week. Meanwhile, Mr. Cross was in the office discussing some updates about my adoption documents with the Andersons, which were nearly complete. This meant I could be living with my new parents very soon.

It was hard to sleep that night, and we sat talking until the early hours of the morning. We slept briefly and were woken up by the bell ringing for breakfast. We got ready quickly and made our way downstairs, passing Miss Crow and Mr. Bates in the hall, who looked at us before going into the office. Holly remarked, "I wonder what they're here for?" During breakfast, Mr. Cross came into the dining room and asked Holly to come to the office with him. She followed him out of the dining room, looking worried. When breakfast ended, she still hadn't returned, so I sat waiting for her until one of the staff came over to me and said, "Holly's gone to see her father. He's in the hospital, but she'll be back later."

She returned later that afternoon with Mr. Cross from the hospital, and he brought her up to the room. He ordered some food to be sent up for her and then left. Once he'd gone, she told me that her father was seriously ill in the hospital and might die. That's why he'd sent for her, to bring her to the hospital. He wanted her to know that if anything happened to him, she would be taken care of. He'd arranged for that to be done through his lawyer with monthly instalments of money from the bank. That night she hardly slept, and the next day Mr. Cross sent for the doctor, who came to see her and gave her some medicine to take for the next few days.

On Sunday, Gran arrived with the Andersons to see us. She asked, "Where's Holly?" I told her about Holly's father being ill in the hospital and that she wasn't well and was upstairs in our room. Gran looked at Mr. Anderson, who got up and left for the office to speak with Mr. Cross. He returned a few minutes later and said to Gran, "You can go upstairs to see Holly." Gran asked me to show them both the way to our room. Mum took my hand, and we went upstairs.

The door of our room was open, and Holly was lying on the bed with her eyes closed. Gran went over to her and tapped her arm. She opened her eyes and began to cry, telling Gran how much she'd missed her. Gran hugged her and said, "Everything's going to get sorted out. Our family's here for you if you need anything." While Gran was talking to her, a draft of air slammed the door shut, and a faint ball of light appeared between them. I wondered if Amanda arranged to get her family upstairs to see Holly. In seconds, the ball of light had gone. Holly seemed better after Gran's visit and came downstairs for dinner that evening.

Over the following days, she gradually returned to normal, and her father's condition didn't get any worse. She seemed to be feeling better and adapting back into our daily routine. On our return to the orphanage after Christmas, we were surprised to find Cora and Oscar still there. They remained an ongoing threat for Holly, as they were always out to make trouble for someone in the orphanage.

As the weather gradually improved, we were allowed to use the garden again with staff on duty all the time since the fight. One morning after breakfast, Mr. Cross asked me to go to the office, as he had something to tell me. When I got to the office, he said, "Sit on that chair. I've got some good news for you about your adoption. The documents are nearly completed, and in them, your name is Sally Jane Anderson. You're four years old and able to talk and read a little." On hearing this news, I replied, "My wish has come true to have parents and a new life." He replied, "You're very lucky, Sally, to be adopted so quickly by the Andersons. That's all for the moment. You can go and join Holly."

I left the office happy, knowing that I'd never have to be anyone's doll again. I'm a girl now. I rushed off to find Holly, who was in the lounge doing her homework, to tell her the good news. After telling her, she seemed pleased about my adoption being nearly completed. She picked me up, swung me around, and said, "That's really great news, Sally. You'll be happy with your new parents and Gran. Your life's never going to be dull." Holly's fifteenth birthday was getting close, and Gran was planning a party for her, which we were both looking forward to.

Chapter 23
Holly's Birthday

On Holly's birthday, the family arrived early as Gran wanted plenty of time to arrange everything for the party. They were taken into the lounge upon arrival, and the door was closed. Mr. Cross put a notice on the lounge door, indicating there was a meeting until 5:30 pm. The Andersons had booked a hotel overnight near the orphanage, and Holly guessed something was up when they mentioned that Gran couldn't make it and handed her a present from her.

The lounge door stayed shut all day with Gran hidden inside until the party. Mum brought a present for me to give Holly, which she was delighted with. When she tore off the wrapping paper and found a beautiful pink dress inside, she exclaimed, "It's gorgeous! Thanks, Sally. I'll wear it tonight for dinner." She kissed me and said, "Why don't you find your mum and show her the garden so you can spend some time together?"

I liked the idea, so I went to look for her and found her standing alone in the hall. She saw me, came over, took my hand, and said, "Soon you'll have to start calling me Mum, Sally, because you'll be coming to live with us. Is that okay with you?" I replied, "Yes, Mum." She giggled, reminding me of Amanda. I squeezed her hand as she opened the door, and we went into the garden. While we were out there, she asked, "Would you like a cat or a dog once you're living with us?" I replied, "I'll have one of each." She giggled again and said, "It's cold out here, let's go back inside." We went indoors, had a warm drink, and I liked having a mother. Mrs. Anderson was going to be mine very soon.

Later that afternoon, I went up to the room and found Holly wearing her new dress, looking pretty. She helped me wash and get ready quickly. Then we went downstairs to join the other kids queuing outside the lounge door. As we arrived, the grandfather clock in the hall struck 5:30 pm. The lounge door opened, with the sound of an orchestra playing "Happy Birthday" floating out of the loudspeakers. Mr. Cross, dressed in Dickensian-style clothes, appeared and told us to go in. The lounge was decorated with banners wishing Holly a happy birthday. She squeezed my hand as we entered and said, "Wow! This is going to be a great birthday. All that's missing is Gran and my father." The tables were laid with a variety of dishes, sandwiches, and desserts. Gran had gone all out arranging this spread for Holly's party.

The birthday music was still playing when Mr. Anderson entered the room with Holly's father in a wheelchair. She was surprised and rushed over to him as Mr. Anderson helped him onto a sofa. She kissed her father and sat next to him. The other kids had never been to a party like Holly's before, as Gran had thought of everything to make it fun and enjoyable for everyone.

Then Gran made her entrance, singing out of tune with a CD playing. She was dressed as Sleeping Beauty, wearing a long blonde wig and a costume far too tight for her. The kids clapped, applauded, and loved her singing as it grew louder and worse. Then she came over to me and asked me to join her. The laughter grew louder as we both sang the rest of the song together, out of tune until it ended. Holly rushed over to Gran to kiss her, and the party continued until the bell rang for bedtime. It was a great success; everyone had a fantastic time playing games, winning prizes, and having fun.

Once the party ended, Holly's father was going to spend the night at the hotel where the Andersons were staying, and they would take him back to his nursing home the following day. Before going up to our room, Holly thanked the Andersons for arranging for her father to be at her birthday party. His gift to her was a mobile phone, which she was thrilled with. Everything seemed to be working out for both of us, and my adoption papers were almost ready. I was looking forward to having the Andersons as my parents but worried about leaving Holly behind once I left the orphanage.

The next few weeks passed quickly, and summer approached with warmer days and some rainy ones. One morning at breakfast, Mr. Cross announced there was going to be another outing. This time he wanted us to choose where we'd like to go. He handed out some leaflets with a list of places and said, "You've got one week to choose where you'd like to go by voting. Once the results are counted, I'll book the coach." The rest of the leaflets were given out, and there was a buzz of excitement and noisy gossip as we left the dining room.

A week later, at breakfast, Mr. Cross said, "The votes have been counted, and Tommy Edwards won with the most votes for Castleton Noir. It's a medieval town close to the sea, famous for its Gothic stories of hauntings and strange tales of giant bats that people claim are vampires in disguise." After his announcement, there was a thunderous round of applause from everyone, and he said, "I'll let you know the date of the outing once I've booked the coach."

This was the last outing I'd make with the kids from the orphanage and the first time we met Duke William Alaric by chance during our visit to Alaric Castle. We didn't know then that he'd become a lifetime friend for my family, Holly, and me through a twist of fate that took place on that outing to Castleton Noir. A few days after that outing, my adoption papers were completed, and I left the orphanage with my new parents, the Andersons.

Chapter 24
The Duke and Alaric Castle

On the day of the outing, it was cloudy and looked like it was going to rain. The coach arrived on time, and after we all boarded it, we left for Castleton Noir, which was a long journey. Upon our arrival, it was raining and dull, with a storm raging in the distance, so we had to sit in the coach until the rain finally stopped. Mr. Cross then made an announcement, saying, "You've got four hours to explore Castletown Noire, and I want everyone back at the coach by 5 PM to leave." That rang a bell for both of us, after our last trip to the forest and getting lost.

Once the coach was parked on the seafront, you had a good view of the town from where we were. With a medieval castle in the background, shrouded in grey mist and dark clouds, that created an air of mystery around the Gothic town. As we walked away from the coach, I noticed the streets were made of cobblestones. We walked down the first main road we came to, which was busy with a large variety of shops, cafés, and even a fish & chip bar where you could have lunch. We'd all been given some money to spend on the outing, so we went to look around some of the different shops first, to buy souvenirs to take back with us.

While we were going in and out of various shops, Holly noticed a tall, smartly dressed man in a dark coat who had stopped outside a shop we were in and was watching us. When we left the shop, he was walking behind us. She mentioned this, saying, "I hope he isn't following us." She turned around to see if he was there, but he had gone. After walking a short distance down that street, she looked again, and the man had reappeared, walking a short distance behind us. I could see this was worrying her when she stopped suddenly and said, "Let's lose him and go to have lunch." We did that and found a small restaurant opposite the park. We sat at a table by the window, which had a good view of the main road and the park. While we were having lunch, the man we thought might be following us passed the restaurant, crossed the main road, and stood by the park entrance to make a phone call on his mobile. We watched him while we ate, and a few minutes after making his call, a large black car arrived, stopped where he was standing, and he got into the car and left, disappearing into the traffic. Once lunch was over, we decided to walk up to the castle and have a look around for ourselves.

Tom, who was on the outing with us, had told us some creepy stories about the castle on the coach and its mysterious history. These consisted of abnormal tales passed down over the centuries about supernatural hauntings taking place in the castle. So, we were curious to see the place for ourselves. People claimed it was haunted, and we wanted to spend time there before catching the coach back to the orphanage.

Auric Castle was situated above the town on a hill, with a steep walk up a winding path to reach it. As we started to walk towards the castle, it began to rain, and a light mist covered our path, gradually becoming thicker as we walked on. While this was happening, Amanda's ghost materialized through the mist and spoke to me, saying, "This is going to be a super adventure, Sally," and then vanished. Holly looked at me, and we both experienced a premonition about the castle we were about to visit. Tom's stories we'd heard on the coach were weird and bizarre, about what went on in the castle in medieval times with its original owner, and extremely frightening. So, we anticipated an exciting afternoon seeing Auric Castle, which was claimed to be haunted.

Both of us began to feel uneasy as we got closer to the castle because there were no people on the path that led to the entrance, we were alone. With the rain pelting down on us and a roar of thunder coming from somewhere in the distance, as we got closer to the castle. Upon reaching the main entrance gate, we purchased a ticket. After doing that, we walked across a large courtyard that had been converted into a car park for visitors. There was a large signpost directing us to a large wooden door with "Entrance" written on it.

Holly pushed the door open, and we went in, finding ourselves standing in a large medieval hall with shields of armour hung on all the walls. Most of the items were antique and original shields used in battles in which Duke Fredrick Alaric had fought in around the world in the 11th century. While we were looking around the hall, a door opened behind us, and the man we'd seen earlier in town came through it, still wearing his overcoat. He came over to us and asked politely, "Are you interested in being shown around the castle?" Holly replied, "Yes, we'd like a guided tour, if that's possible?" He replied, "It will be a pleasure to show you both around the castle."

While he was talking, we noticed his height and appearance. He was a handsome man in his forties, with silver grey hair tied neatly back in a knot and bluish eyes that were quite hypnotic, as though he knew what you were thinking in modern-day terms, telepathic. There was an air of mystery about this man, as though he belonged to another time and place. He was the type of man you see in medieval paintings in museums, dressed for war in full battle armour.

After a brief silence, Holly asked, "Are the stories true about the original owner of the castle, Duke Fredrick Alaric?" He replied, "Very few of the stories are anywhere near the truth." She said, "How do we really know? We weren't there." He was silent, then said, "Most of the stories were created from rumours, but the ones about the castle being haunted are true. There are various hauntings that have continued throughout the centuries, with the spirits of people who lived and died in the castle, experiencing tragic deaths." Holly replied, "I thought most of the stories were created for publicity, to capture people's imagination to visit the castle." He said, "Let me

94

give you an idea of what life was like in medieval times, with an insight into the stories connected to the castle."

He then began to narrate his version of the duke's life, as though he'd known him personally, with a believable account of what he was like. He began by saying, "The duke didn't have a bad character, but he inherited a strange abnormality that was passed onto him through his ancestor's bloodline, which he was obligated to live with. This created wild rumours about the duke that spread throughout Castleton Noir. This gossip accused the duke of indulging in freakish behaviours and being able to shapeshift into a strange fiendish beast that prowled the town when darkness descended on Castleton Noir.

The beast would then search for a victim to drain their body and life force, leaving the victim lifeless. Through the hearsay going on, the duke was branded a vampire. To end the rumours, he left the castle and his family behind to become a knight. He fought with King Richard the Lionheart in the Crusades of Jerusalem, living a solitary life as a soldier.

The duke's life altered after visiting Italy on his way back to England after the Crusades in the Holy Land. On that visit to Italy, he met his future wife while staying with Duke Moretti's family and met their daughter Giovanna. She had a sweet nature and the beauty of a porcelain doll, with long dark auburn hair, an oval-shaped face, and large hazel brown eyes. After meeting Giovanna, the duke fell head over heels in love with her, and they became inseparable. But there was a problem Giovanna had already been promised in marriage by her family to another nobleman's son, which both families wanted to take place. So, the duke remained in Italy for several months until he finally persuaded her family to give their permission for him to marry Giovanna.

Their wedding was a grand affair with hundreds of guests and took place in Venice. The couple then spent their honeymoon in Paris, and after their visit to France, the duke returned to England with his new bride to live in the castle. They were a perfect match and happy together there for many years until his wife's death. He mourned Giovanna for many years after her passing and lived the remaining years of his life like a recluse in the castle, remembering the happy years they'd spent together before her death.

During those years together, he continued to suffer from the attacks that took control of his body at various times. He learned to control them in an orderly manner, locking himself in the strong room of the castle for days until the condition passed. Giovanna was his entire world, and the thought of harming her plagued him. During the duke's lifetime, he never stopped searching for an answer to be set free from the abomination he inherited from his family.

Throughout the years prior to her death, rumours never stopped circulating, with horrifying stories about them both spreading like wildfire. These stories reached English nobility and Europe, branding the duke as a vampire. Books were written centuries later about the duke being a vampire, and many horror movies were made about his life and family. He became an icon of horror, transformed into a bloodthirsty vampire, which destroyed his reputation. No one knew or understood what his life was really like, suffering from the constant turmoil of the condition he desperately attempted to control, which was soul-destroying.

Duke Frederick loathed the word vampire, and Giovanna would sit crying about what people were saying about them. The man with us seemed quite affected by the duke's tragic story when he asked, "Do you want to see the rest of the castle?" Holly replied, "Yes, if that's okay with you." Then we followed him down a long corridor, where he stopped in front of an ornate oak door, opened it, and showed us into a large room full of books arranged on shelves around the walls, being used as a library. The room was decorated in Victorian style, with soft velvet wallpaper in a pale shade of red and a few paintings edged with gold hung on the walls.

In the centre of the room, there was a large marble fireplace, and above it on the wall hung a painting of a man dressed in full Crusader armour with a sword. He looked exactly like the man with us, who was showing us around the castle. The resemblance was astounding. Holly asked, "Who's the man in the painting?" He replied, "That's my ancestor, Duke Fredrick Alaric. I'm Duke William Alaric." I said, "You're identical and could be twins." He smiled, bent down, and whispered to me, "Keep my secret, I'll keep yours, little doll."

Holly looked at her watch and said, "What would you recommend we see next? We don't have much time." He replied, "The catacombs under the castle, where some of my ancestors are buried." She looked nervous after he mentioned going under the castle, and I felt scared when he said, "We don't usually take visitors down there. I'm breaking the rules, letting you see the catacombs." I thought, "We've just met this man and shouldn't be going anywhere with him without someone knowing where he was taking us." Out of nowhere, Amanda materialized next to the duke and gave me the thumbs up, which meant we were in the middle of an adventure.

Holly didn't reply about going under the castle. The duke sensed what we were thinking and said, "There are cameras under the castle. Does that make you feel safer, or would you like me to call one of the staff to let them know we're going down there?" We both nodded. He pressed a buzzer, and a lady arrived, whom he introduced as his housekeeper. He told her that we were going down to the catacombs and wouldn't be long. Then he said, "Why are you frightened of me? I'd never harm either of you." After an awkward silence, he said, "You don't have to see the catacombs, it's up to you." We looked at each other, and Holly replied, "We'd like to see them," although she still felt somewhat uneasy. We then followed him to a large door that opened onto a small landing with a flight of stairs that led down to the catacombs.

Still following the duke, we made our way down the stairs into the semi-darkness under the castle. There were lights placed equally around the walls, and he walked ahead of us holding a torch. He stopped suddenly, turned around, and said to Holly, "Please don't be afraid of me. I'm taking you to see someone special whose tomb is down here, which the public aren't allowed to see." We continued following him, wondering whose burial place we were about to see until he stopped in front of an ornate marble tomb with a statue of a lady carved on top of it. A peculiar silence covered the area surrounding the tomb as we stood next to it.

Then he began to speak, saying, "The lady buried in the tomb is Giovanna Alaric, Duke Frederick's beloved wife." After explaining what caused her tragic death, he became withdrawn and silent. An overwhelming scent of flowers covered the tomb. He touched the statue and seemed to sense the spirit of Giovanna, that centuries and time couldn't erase. After a short silence, he continued with their story, saying, "The people of Castleton Noire were very superstitious in medieval times and thought the duke's wife was a shape-shifter who could change from a bat into a vampire, as there were many bats flying around the castle at night. Also, a number of mysterious deaths had taken place in the rural part of Castleton Noir, which were unresolved.

The townspeople were looking for someone to blame for the brutal murders. As gossip spread in the town about the duke and his wife being vampires, Giovanna was chosen as the perpetrator of the murders and had to be killed. She was innocent, and her death was planned and carried out by one of the servants who worked in the kitchen of the castle. He was being paid by someone to gradually poison her when he served their meals each day. The duke was worried about his wife's failing health a few weeks before her death and had already arranged for her to see a specialist in London the week she died.

Giovanna took her last walk around the castle grounds the day before she died, in the morning with her dogs, and collapsed in the garden. She was taken upstairs to their apartment in the castle. A doctor was sent for, who said it might be some sort of food poisoning caused by something she'd eaten, as she was experiencing stomach cramps and bleeding. The duke stayed with his wife all night until the following morning when she died in his arms. Heartbroken and devastated, he stayed in their apartment with her and wouldn't let anyone come near Giovanna. He attended to everything himself, not allowing any of the castle staff to come near her. He grieved endlessly for months after her death, as she was his entire world that he lived for.

During the months after her death, the servants said they used to hear him crying out to God, 'Why have you done this to us?' The duke with us looked towards the tomb and said, 'This mausoleum was built especially for her, and the duke carried Giovanna down to the catacombs and buried her himself. He stayed with her for several days alone in the catacombs.' Following her death, malicious gossip didn't stop but continued in Castleton Noire. Rumours of the duke being able to transform into a beastly creature at night that prowled the town looking for a victim to devour, came about through people hearing his anguished cries that echoed from the castle through the streets of the town. The cries the townspeople heard and gossiped about were for his wife's tragic death and the despair he felt without her in his life.

The reason Giovanna wasn't buried in the family vault in the cemetery was that the duke knew people would desecrate her resting place. He'd loved her in life, and death couldn't separate them. That's why she was buried in the catacombs under the castle for safety, so nothing evil could touch her. Another reason was that the duke felt lost without her and wanted her to remain close to him while he lived.

Throughout the years that followed, the duke continued to visit various doctors in England and Europe, looking for a cure to be set free from the curse that eventually touched both of their lives. Duke Frederick had a persistent nature and never stopped searching for an answer to solve the problem that had devoured his life through his ancestor's bloodline. Strange morbid stories are still being told about them both, centuries after their deaths.

The tragedy of Duke Frederick's life seemed to have a shattering effect on the duke with us. He was still standing by the tomb in silence, touched it again, sighed, and said, "Let's go back upstairs, young ladies." We followed him upstairs to the main entrance hall. He stood looking lost in his thoughts for a few seconds, then remarked, "Everyone has secrets, don't we, sweetie?" After a brief silence, he took a heart-shaped locket out of the inside pocket of his jacket, opened it, and showed it to us. There was a cameo painting inside the locket of an extremely beautiful lady with perfect features. We said together, "The lady's gorgeous." He replied, "That's Giovanna, Duke Frederick's wife. I treasure this souvenir that belonged to the duke, as they say he always carried it with him after his wife's death."

He continued speaking, "I saw you both in town this morning and thought you might visit the castle. Then saw you come into the main hall on the security cameras and thought I'd show you both around my home myself." Holly asked, "Don't you have staff to do that?" He replied, "Yes, I do, but this time I couldn't resist doing the tourist guide bit myself. I hope you've enjoyed your visit, it's been an interesting one for me, showing you around the castle."

Then he asked, "Would you like to have afternoon tea before you leave to catch your coach? There's a cafeteria in the garden area. I'll show you where it is." He took us through the garden to a modern cafeteria and said, "I have a few things to do, and I will come back to see you both before you leave." We were shown to a table by staff and had full afternoon tea. The duke returned while we were still eating, ordered a cup of tea, and sat chatting with us until Holly said, "Put your coat on, Sally. We have to go, or we will be late for the coach."

The duke stood up and said, "I need some fresh air. I'll walk to the main entrance gate of the castle with you both." He shook hands with us and said, "I hope everything works out for you both with your lives. Come to visit the castle again when you can, and keep in touch with your news." Then he spoke to Holly and said, "You've been a good friend to this little girl when she needed one. I hope your friendship lasts throughout your lives. Have a safe journey back to the orphanage."

Once we reached the main entrance gate of the castle, the duke remained standing there as we made our way back down the winding path, still covered in light mist. Halfway down the path, we turned around and could see the duke faintly through the mist by the entrance gate, and he waved. The mist remained with us until we reached the main road, where our adventure had begun that day when we took a walk up the winding path to the castle.

Our coach was still parked on the seafront, and there was a large bat hanging upside down on a tree opposite where the coach was parked until we left. The bat flew alongside the coach for half of the journey back to the orphanage, then vanished! Auric Castle was the second outing I'd been on that had turned into another weird adventure of hidden mysteries that Amanda would have loved to be part of. Meeting the duke in person left me with a strange feeling that I'd be returning to the castle and seeing him again in the future. This did happen at a later date, as Holly kept in touch with him, and eventually, he became a friend to both of us and my new parents, and an important figure of help when needed in our lives. Holly made a prediction that day with a remark as we got on the coach, when she said, "I've got a feeling we'll be coming back here one day. I don't know why."

Chapter 25
Leaving the Orphanage

The last week I spent at the orphanage passed quickly, with our usual daily routine continuing until the Sunday when the Andersons arrived early to see me. I was having lunch with Holly in the dining room when Mr. Cross came in and asked me to go to the lounge once I'd finished eating, as the Andersons were waiting for me there. After lunch, Holly went upstairs to write to her father, and I went to the lounge.

As I opened the lounge door, my future mum came rushing over to me, picked me up, and hugged me saying, "We've got your adoption papers, Sally. You're our daughter now," and began to cry. Mr. Anderson came over, took me from her, and sat me on the couch next to mum. She said, "You can come home with us today, Sally. I've been so worried about you living so far away from us," hugging me again.

My wish to be a girl had come true, along with having a mother who loved me. My transformation from a doll into a girl had been a journey full of adventures, culminating in being adopted, gaining parents, and a home. While I was sitting on mum's lap, the lounge door opened. Mr. Cross came back into the room and asked the Andersons, "Would you like someone to pack Sally's things so she can leave with you this afternoon?" Dad replied, "Yes, if that can be done, but first I must speak to Holly, as I've got a message from her father for her."

Holly was sent for and joined us in the lounge. Mr. Anderson spoke to her, saying, "Your father's health has improved, and he is planning to get a flat in sheltered accommodation, so you can go to live with him." Holly was overwhelmed with the news and the possibility of leaving the orphanage to live with her father. Dad continued speaking, saying, "You'll always be welcome to stay with us or Gran whenever you have free time." Tearfully, she said, "I guess you'll be leaving this afternoon with your parents." She tried to look cheerful and said, "Come on, Sally, let's go and get your things packed. You're going home today." Mr. Cross smiled at her and said, "Thanks, can you help her pack her things? The Andersons want to take her home with them this afternoon." Holly took my hand, and we made our way upstairs. Once we reached our room, she began packing my things into large bags, trying not to cry while doing this. She said, "I'll miss you, Sally. We've been through a lot together since you arrived here."

I'll never forget that Sunday when I left the orphanage with my new parents and said goodbye to everyone. I knew I'd be seeing Holly the following weekend, as my parents had already invited her. Since my arrival at the orphanage with Miss Crow, I'd experienced many different things being with other children every day, things I still talk about with Holly whenever we meet. Our friendship has lasted over the years. Mr. Cross was pleased about me being adopted by the Andersons, knowing I'd have a good home to grow up in. I wanted to cry when the time came to say goodbye to him. As I was about to leave with my new parents, he gave me a hug. I was going to miss him.

The kids at the orphanage gave me a doll named Sandy, with bright red hair, who looked strangely like Amanda. When mum saw me holding the doll, she giggled, grabbed her from me, saying, "I want her before she starts getting up to her tricks," and hugged the doll. I renamed my doll Amanda, as we'd both be sharing her bedroom, which was now mine. Spending time with the other children in the orphanage had taught me a great deal about life as a girl. You have to adapt and learn various things about other kids' behaviour when they are orphans and don't have parents.

When the time came to leave, all the children I'd known in the orphanage came outside to wave goodbye. Holly walked to the car with us, gave me a hug, and said, "Your adventures here have ended, and a new one's about to begin. I'll see you next weekend. Stay out of trouble." She kissed my parents, and I got into the car with mum while dad put my bags and case into the boot of the car. As he was doing this, a misty vision of Amanda appeared by the car, blew me a kiss, then vanished. As we drove away from the orphanage, leaving it behind in the distance, I realized that everything I'd wished for had come true.

The journey home with my new parents was the beginning of a new life for me as the Andersons' daughter, living in Whispering Echoes, their home. My transformation into a girl had shown me that an impossible wish could come true. Although coming back to live in the house where I'd been Amanda's doll might have its setbacks, as her ghost knew my secret. As we drove on through the afternoon, getting closer to home, memories came flooding back from the past of our adventures together in the attic.

We'd seen many strange ghostly manifestations and weird apparitions once Amanda opened the door and went into the attic. We found ourselves in the supernatural world that lay up there, behind the closed attic door. What we saw each time we went up there was scary, terrifying, and totally unbelievable. That could still be going on until someone removes the strange paranormal activities in the attic.

It was a long drive home, filled with memories of everything that happened since Gran found me in Amanda's bed when I'd changed into a small girl. The explanation people were given was that I'd been left there by someone, which was accepted. I was frightened when Miss Crow took me away from the Andersons to the orphanage, but met Holly on my arrival, who became my friend, eased my fear. Being adopted by Amanda's parents was giving me the chance for a new life after my previous existence as their daughter's doll, which had to remain a secret.

How could I forget Amanda's tragic death, or her father buying me from the charity shop for her as a present? Since that time, our lives had reversed, and now he was going to be my father. My transformation into a human girl is a strange story for anyone to believe. It's interesting but weird for anyone to accept, but it happened to me.

Being someone's doll was an experience of both love and hatred. I'm lucky to have found kind parents like the Andersons who've adopted me. What's changed for Amanda and me are our identities, now I'm a girl, and she's a ghost, which she doesn't like being. I discovered this shortly after my arrival in my new home with my parents. I began to feel that I was being watched, and doors started slamming shut suddenly, leaving the room freezing cold. This began happening frequently, and realized what life was going to be like living in a haunted house with a resident ghost who wanted attention. She began haunting the house with morbid noises to frighten me.

Using her ghostly powers to seek revenge against her family for adopting me, as I'd replaced her position as the Andersons' daughter. We're nearly home, and I'll let you know what happens once I'm living in Whispering Echoes with my new parents.

I'd appreciate a review to promote this first book in the series, if you've enjoyed reading it, thank you. Irene Martinez.

www.ingramcontent.com/pod-product-compliance
Lightning Source LLC
Chambersburg PA
CBHW071331130626
46556CB00004B/1853